ONLY HIS

(A Sadie Price FBI Suspense Thriller—Book 3)

Rylie Dark

Rylie Dark

Debut author Rylie Dark is author of the SADIE PRICE FBI SUSPENSE THRILLER series, comprising six books (and counting); the MIA NORTH FBI SUSPENSE THRILLER series, comprising three books (and counting); and the CARLY SEE FBI SUSPENSE THRILLER, comprising three books (and counting).

An avid reader and lifelong fan of the mystery and thriller genres, Rylie loves to hear from you, so please feel free to visit www.ryliedark.com to learn more and stay in touch.

ISBN: 978-1-0943-7595-3

CHAPTER ONE

This had been a long time coming.

Sadie banged on the door of her father's rundown cabin as loud as she could, and then stood back and waited. In her other hand, she held the folder that Sheriff Cooper had given her before she had left the station. She had a lot of questions for her father.

Getting him to answer them honestly, however, now that was another thing.

"Who is it?" his voice yelled, just as Sadie saw the curtain in the window twitch. He knew damn well that it was her. She answered him anyway.

"It's me, Dad," she yelled, although the word stuck in her throat. He had long ago lost the right to be called that by her. "It's Sadie."

There was silence. She banged the door again. "I'm not going anywhere," she yelled, "until you answer this goddamn door."

Finally, she heard his footsteps coming toward the door, and she held herself still as she heard the bolts slide back. For just a second, she was a frightened kid again, fearing the wrath of her father but determined not to show it. Then she took a deep breath, and the moment passed.

She wasn't a kid anymore. She was an FBI special agent, an expert in her field in the Behavioral Analysis Unit who had gotten further and achieved more than her father would have ever believed her capable, and she had done it alone and without his help. There was nothing to be scared of anymore.

At least, that was what she told herself.

When the door cracked open and his face appeared, her first thought was how ill he looked. She knew that he had terminal cancer, and right now it showed, He had lost weight, his skin was wrinkly and tinged with gray, and his eyes were rheumy with bloodshot irises.

She could smell the booze on him too. Some things never changed.

For all his pitiful appearance, however, his eyes burned with something like his old malevolence, causing Sadie to stiffen, preventing herself from taking an instinctive step back. She'd be damned before she would show the mean old bastard any fear.

"I told you last time to go away," he said, spitting out his words.

1

Sadie stood her ground. "Sorry, Dad, no can do. I need to talk to you, and you are going to talk to me. It's been too long."

He snorted. "Not long enough. What are you doing back here? I saw you in the news," he added, but his tone was accusatory, as though he thought she had returned simply to spite him.

Perhaps, on some level, she had.

"I had a job to do."

"Go and do it, then," he spat. "What do you want with me? Turning up here after all this time, after no word for years."

Sadie shook her head, wondering just what story he was telling himself where he had somehow managed to end up as the victim in their family situation. She didn't have time for this.

"I'm not here about me and you, Dad," she said. "I have questions to ask you. And if I have to haul your ass down to Sheriff Cooper's station to get you to answer them, then I swear to God that's exactly what I'll do."

He glared at her, but Sadie met his gaze head on. He went to slam the door in her face once again, but this time Sadie was expecting it and was too quick for him. He looked down in surprise at Sadie's leather-booted foot wedged in between the door and the frame.

"Let me in," she said. He stared at her with hatred and, she was amazed to see, even fear in his eyes.

Then, to her surprise, he opened the door.

Well, that was easier than I expected, she thought to herself as she stepped into the small cabin.

It hadn't changed much since the last time she had been here, before she left for college and the FBI, over a decade ago. When she had been an anxious and rebellious teenager, desperate to get away from Alaska and the memories of her childhood.

Memories of Jessica.

There was no trace of her dead sister in the cabin. No pictures, nothing that had once belonged to her. It was odd, because Jessica had been her father's favorite daughter, but then he had never had pictures of their mother up, either.

"I've come about Jessica, Dad," she said, deciding that to cut to the chase would be the best tactic.

He ignored her, turning his back on her and walking through into the small kitchen. "Coffee?" he barked at her, loudly rattling around. Sadie followed him inside.

"Please. Make it strong." She watched him as he puttered around, noticing how much his movements had slowed and the way he winced when he lifted the kettle onto the gas ring. She knew better than to offer him any help, but it was hard not to feel a twinge of sympathy.

"I heard you were ill," she said carefully. He stopped what he was doing and looked over his scrawny shoulder to glare at her.

"So they say. I don't have much faith in doctors." He banged a cup down on the counter, making it clear it wasn't a subject that he had any intention of discussing.

Sadie didn't pursue it. His illness wasn't why she was here.

He carried the coffees back through to the main room and she followed him, sitting down on the beaten old sofa and taking the hot mug from him. He sat at the table, looking relieved to be off his feet.

"What brought you back?" he asked, and it sounded more like a challenge than a question born out of genuine interest.

"Work," Sadie said shortly. "It was time for a change. I got sick of Washington."

She had no intention of talking about her last case in DC, the events of which she was still processing. A man had ended up dead, and Sadie was still waiting to be recalled for the inquiry. It would have happened already, but her recent hospital stay over Christmas had postponed it to a date that was yet to be issued.

Then there was Jessica. Her sister's memory had been calling her back for some time. Sadie had never believed that her older sibling's drowning had been accidental, and a recent discovery had made it clear that her father may know more about that than he had ever told her.

"You've done well for yourself," he said, and she blinked rapidly, trying not to show her amazement. There was no bitterness in his voice, but a faint tinge of pride.

He had never been proud of her. She couldn't remember a time when he hadn't made it clear that his younger daughter was surplus to requirements. After her mother had died of cancer when she was a little kid, his indifference had turned into downright hostility. As his drinking had progressed, the physical abuse had started.

After Jessica's death, he never even seemed to notice that she was there, instead retreating further and further into the bottle.

"Thanks," she muttered. There was an awkward silence, during which they both stared at the floor.

Sadie took a deep breath. This wasn't how she had imagined things going. She had expected him to shout, or even threaten her with a firearm—it wouldn't be the first time—but not this.

She opened the folder on her lap and told herself that it was time to get some answers.

3

"Sheriff Cooper is helping me take a look back over Jessica's case. And there a few things I need to ask you."

His eyes narrowed. "Are you here to interrogate me?" he said, the anger back in his voice. "You never could leave things alone. Even as a kid you were always nosing around and asking questions. I should have known you would end up a cop."

Here we go, Sadie thought. This was the father she was used to. This guy, she knew how to deal with.

"There are discrepancies, Dad," she pressed. "I've never believed that she just drowned, it was never investigated properly. The sheriff agrees. We're opening it up as a cold case."

Her father's hands clenched into fists at his sides. Sadie held his gaze, keeping her cool. "Don't think of getting physical, Dad," she warned him, her voice like steel. "You're an old man now, and I'm a trained FBI agent. Do yourself a favor and don't act on that temper."

He looked furious and for a moment she was waiting for him to come at her, but then she saw his fists unclench. An expression that could even have been a smile tugged at the corner of his mouth.

"I heard you broke Ted's boy's nose in the saloon a few weeks ago," he said. This time there was no mistaking the pride in his voice. She wondered who had told him. Her father was practically a recluse these days, but word traveled fast around here, even if the cabins got farther and farther apart the deeper you traveled away from Anchorage and out into the hinterlands.

"It was self-defense." She shrugged. She wasn't going to lose any sleep over it; the guy was a creep who had tried to grope her at the bar during a routine inquiry. He had deserved it.

Her father took a deep swig of his coffee, and the awkward silence descended again. Sadie knew she was unlikely to get much out of him, but she had to try. Whatever it was that her father knew about Jessica's death could be the key to the whole case.

"When Jessica went missing," she went on, "you made a call to nine one one."

"Well, of course I did," he snapped. "Who else would I call?"

"Sheriff Cooper found the original transcription of that call." She pulled the transcript out of the folder and held it out for him to see. He didn't take it and she pulled her hand back, leaving the transcription face up on her lap. She looked down at it, making sure she had the words right. A chill went through her as she repeated them.

"You didn't just say that she hadn't been back all night, Dad," she said slowly. "You said, 'They took her.' Who? Who did you think had taken her?"

Her father's face had gone gray, and he wheezed when he spoke. Although his eyes were as hard as gimlets, she could see a faint sheen of sweat on his brow and she knew that her question had unsettled him. He knew something.

And she wasn't leaving until she knew what it was.

"I don't remember saying that," he snapped, not meeting her eyes. "They must have misheard me. Or maybe they wrote it down wrong."

"You were questioned about it by the local sheriff at the time," Sadie went on, "and you said the same thing then. That you didn't remember. Because you were drunk." She refrained from adding her immediate thought, which was that her father had nearly always been drunk.

"Well, there you go." He sat back and crossed his arms. "There's your answer."

"Except," Sadie countered, "I remember that morning, Dad. You had been asleep. You hadn't had any more alcohol the night before than usual. You must have known what you were saying, so that doesn't make sense."

"I was in shock," he said stubbornly. "I was worried about your sister. You hear all sorts of things about young girls being kidnapped by some psychopath. You should know all about that, in your job."

"Oh, I do." Sadie nodded. "But you weren't what I would call an overly anxious parent, were you? You left us to fend for ourselves all the time. And around here, most people would assume an accident or even a wild animal before they would consider a kidnap. Or even just that she was being rebellious, out with a boyfriend or something."

"She wouldn't have done that. Because she wouldn't leave you on your own." He didn't say the words *with me*, but they hung in the air between them.

"No, she wouldn't," Sadie said softly. She looked away, feeling the threat of tears behind her eyes. Two years older, Jessica had always put herself between their father and her younger sister. Jessica had been the only person who could sometimes talk him down from one of his rages.

Sadie had loved her older sister with a passion. Her death had left a void in Sadie's life that had never been filled, and now that her hunger for justice for her sister's death had been reawakened, she knew she wouldn't fully rest again until she knew the truth.

5

"I don't believe you, Dad," she said firmly, meeting his eyes again. "You wouldn't have said that without a good reason. If you thought someone had taken her, then you suspected that they had. And there would be no reason for you to think that unless you had someone in mind."

Sadie leaned forward in her seat, feeling the adrenaline rise as it always did when she was on a case.

This time, though, it was personal.

"You thought you knew, didn't you?" she pressed, staring at her father now with unblinking eyes. He visibly shuddered under her gaze, and she knew she was getting to him. "You suspected someone—or more than one person, because you said 'they'—of taking her. *Who*, Dad? Why haven't you said anything all these years? Are you scared of them?"

Her dad slumped in his chair, looking defeated, and when he opened his mouth to speak Sadie felt a brief flicker of triumph. She had him.

But then the moment was over, and he was on his feet, towering over her just like he had years ago, his features twisted in rage.

"How dare you!" he yelled, spittle flying from the corners of his mouth. "Turning up here after all these years, thinking you can order me around and stick your nose in where it's not wanted. Jessica is dead, do you hear me! Dead!"

Sadie got slowly to her feet, feeling her whole body burning with a fury to match his own.

"How dare *you*," she said, her voice low and dangerous. "Jessica was my sister! While you were drowning yourself in drink, I was the one who had to live with what happened to her. To carry it all these years, never getting any answers, never knowing if there was anything I could have done to prevent it...to save her. And this whole time you knew something? And never said? If you don't answer me, I will drag your ass down to the station and you can answer me and the sheriff there, on record."

They were eye to eye, glaring at each other, Sadie's whole body trembling with anger and hatred and, underneath it all, grief. For her sister, for the child she herself had been, and for the father he could have been, if the drink hadn't taken over.

It was her father who gave in, sinking back down into his chair. "Okay," he muttered. "I'll try my best."

Holding her breath, Sadie sat opposite him, the anger draining from her and hope taking its place.

"Thank you, Dad," she whispered.

He opened his mouth, but when he tried to speak, his expression seemed to freeze, his mouth contorting. Only a thin wheeze came out, and he grabbed his chest, slumping to the side.

Sadie jumped to her feet, rushing over to his side. "Dad, what is it?" She knelt down next to him and pulled her cell out of her pocket to call for an ambulance.

Her father was going into cardiac arrest.

CHAPTER TWO

If there was one feeling Sadie hated more than any other, it was feeling helpless. As she hovered next to her father's bedside in the ICU, watching the doctor and nurse take his vitals once again, a heavy sense of powerlessness settled over her.

Her father had been unconscious by the time the air ambulance arrived. Although his cabin wasn't as deep in the hinterlands as some, recent snowstorms meant that driving over land would have wasted precious time. She had watched them lift up his body as she had climbed into her snow truck, and the sight of him, so small and frail, had brought tears to her eyes.

When she had heard about the cancer, there had been no real emotion. There was no love lost between them. Sadie knew that if he died now, she wouldn't grieve the way she had for her mother and Jessica. What, after all, would she have really lost? Yet for one long moment as she watched him being airlifted to the hospital, she had felt a sharp ache in her heart. Perhaps not so much for what she might lose as for what she had never had.

The sound of machines beeping filled the room. The machines that were currently keeping him alive. The doctor looked at Sadie with sympathy in his eyes, which made her almost flinch away from his gaze. She didn't need pity.

She needed answers.

"What's going to happen to him?"

The doctor smiled sadly. A tall, thin man in his fifties, he looked tired, as though he hadn't slept for days. His name tag read *Dr. Bailey*.

"His condition is stable, but at the moment that is really all that we can tell you. It's a waiting game at this stage, I'm afraid. Thankfully, the CPR you performed on him managed to restart his heart quite quickly. You saved your father's life, Ms. Price."

She didn't know how to respond to that. Her training had taken over, and it had barely registered that it was her own father she was trying to help. She wondered how he would feel when he came around, knowing that she had saved him. She strongly suspected he would resent any notion that he owed anything to her.

If he came around, she reminded herself as the doctor went on.

"At this stage he could be comatose for days—even weeks. There could be brain damage due to the lack of oxygen reaching the brain while his heart was stopped. We won't be able to tell the extent of that until he wakes up."

"So, he will wake up?" Sadie pounced on his last words, but the doctor shook his head.

"As I said, at this stage it's a waiting game. He is stable, so I would hope so, but what we have to remember here is how fragile your father already was. His cancer is very advanced, and he was refusing treatment. We can only hope that his body holds up. There are no guarantees," he finished softly.

Sadie didn't reply but stared down at her father. He looked dead already, his lips blue and his cheeks sunken in and hollowed. Only the steady beeping of the machine indicated the fact that he was still alive.

"If you want to go home, Ms. Price," the doctor said, "we will call you at once if anything changes."

Sadie nodded dully, picking up her bag and moving past the nurse with no more than a quick nod of her head. She felt drained of energy and walked down the corridor of the ICU almost as though she was in a trance.

She was in shock. Not just at the sudden arrest of her father's heart, but at the fact that he had actually agreed to talk to her.

She had been so close.

Not quite ready to leave, she took herself to the small cafeteria and ordered a strong, sugary coffee, taking a seat in a corner booth where she could be alone with her thoughts. Sipping at her coffee and feeling some semblance of life return to her limbs, she stared down at the folder that now lay on the table in front of her.

Her father had been about to tell her what he knew, she was certain of it. She had finally been on the edge solving the mystery of her sister's death, only to have it snatched away at the last minute.

She could almost be angry at him, if it wasn't for the fact that Sadie knew she must have contributed to the cardiac arrest. She had pushed him too far and too fast, making him angry and distressed. His system clearly hadn't been able to cope with it.

But at the same time, Sadie knew that no other approach would have gotten anywhere with him. Appealing to empathy or a finer sensibility that he didn't have would have been worse than useless.

There was nothing she could do now but wait and hope her father would come around, and that when he did, he would still be willing to talk to her.

Or even be capable of it. If he died or had severe brain damage, then whatever he had been about to say would be lost forever.

Sadie put her head in her hands as a sense of despair threatened to overwhelm her. To get so close to the truth only to have it vanish in front of her eyes felt like more than she could bear.

Her phone rang, the loud noise making her jolt in her seat.

It was the sheriff.

"Hey," Sadie answered weakly.

"Everything okay, Price?" Cooper had known she had planned to visit her father today. Over the past few weeks, their relationship had changed from one of wary suspicion to…something else? Mutual respect, certainly, and maybe even friendship. There were also those times she was sure she had caught the sheriff looking at her in a way that signified something more.

She quashed that thought. Sheriff Cooper was a colleague. Work and personal life didn't mix. Not that Sadie had any personal life to speak of.

"I… don't know," she said, not yet ready to talk about the morning's events. When it became apparent that she wasn't going to elaborate, the sheriff cleared his throat, changing the subject rather than pushing her.

"I was calling to see if you wanted to accompany me on a call-out. It's not your usual scene though; sounds like a straightforward bear attack. But I thought you might want to look it over and check that nothing is being missed."

Sadie couldn't help but smile to herself. Mutual respect or not, Cooper was the local sheriff and no happier about having an FBI agent accompany him anywhere than any local cop would be. She knew he was doing this in case she needed an "out" from whatever was going on with her dad.

"Give me the coordinates," she told him. "I'll meet you there."

"Great," he said. "Just to warn you, though, Price; it ain't pretty."

*

The victim's cabin was nestled among the pine trees at the bottom of the mountain. A pretty lodge rather than the ramshackle affair of her father's, it was the winter home of a local writer, Marie DuVale, who had made a name for herself writing bonkbusters full of sand and sea and sex, a far cry from her native home of Alaska.

Sadie had never met her, but she instantly recognized the name. The woman stayed alone up here in the winter, writing. Now it seemed she had fallen victim to a rogue bear attack.

As Sadie jumped out of her truck and trudged toward the cabin, she thought about that. Bear attacks, even deaths, did occasionally happen up here, but it was usually hunters or trappers who were intruding on their turf. It wasn't unheard of for bears to sniff around the cabins, but Sadie couldn't remember having heard of anyone being killed in their own home before, although something similar had happened in Canada a few years ago.

Before she entered the cabin, she wrapped her scarf around her mouth and nose and braced herself for what she might be about to see. She was used to dead bodies, even horrifically mutilated ones, but she had never seen the aftermath of a wild animal attack before, and she wasn't sure what to expect.

The smell of blood hit her before she was even through the doorway.

It was everywhere. Up the walls, splattered on the counters of the small breakfast bar, all over the expensive pine furniture and all over the body itself.

Although, she thought as she steadied herself against a wave of nausea, it wasn't so much a body as pieces of one.

Sheriff Cooper and Pete, the medical examiner, were already there. Pete was cataloging and bagging body parts and for a moment Sadie was surprised. Why wasn't he waiting for Forensics? But then she reminded herself that this wasn't a murder.

"I did warn you it wasn't pretty," Cooper said by way of greeting, sounding apologetic. If this was his way of trying to rescue her from her father, she thought, then it left a lot to be desired.

"Who found her?" she asked.

"A local trapper, Bobby Carson. He's around the back having a smoke. He's pretty shook up, as you can imagine."

Sadie nodded as she looked around the cabin, trying not to make it obvious that she was avoiding looking at the arm that lay a foot to her side in a mass of blood and guts. The bear sure was a messy eater.

There were pictures of Marie and various guys on the shelf, and an award for Best Novelist from some romance authors guild.

"My wife read her books, you know," Pete said sadly. "She will be devastated by this."

"Such a waste of a life," Sadie agreed, although she didn't personally know the author. Although what had happened to the woman was clearly terrible, Sadie didn't feel the outrage and drive for justice that she did when it was a murder victim. Bears were animals, after all, and this one had just done what she guessed hungry bears did, even if it did seem like a particularly savage attack.

She heard a small cough behind her and turned to see a man come in. He was tanned and lean and seemed little affected by the scene of carnage all around them.

"You're Bobby Carson," she said. He saw her badge and his eyes went wide, which was the reaction she was used to when a local realized that she was FBI and not just another state trooper.

Those who didn't know her, anyway. The locals who remembered her as a kid were usually just shocked to see her back.

"You've been on TV," Carson said to her, sounding a little starstruck. "You caught that serial killer."

Sadie still had to get used to her growing reputation as something of a local celebrity. She wondered how Marie DuVale had dealt with that.

"What do you make of this, Bobby?" she asked, ignoring his comment. Bobby looked around and shrugged in distaste.

"Nasty attack, but it does happen. The problem is, now that this bear has gotten a taste for sniffing around cabins and making a meal out of the inhabitants, it's likely to strike again. Once they get a taste for human flesh, they will seek it out."

Sadie winced at the thought of a rogue bear lumbering around the hinterlands. Maybe even making its way down into town, lured by the promise of rich pickings.

"I guess a bear hunt is needed?" she asked. Cooper nodded.

"I've got a fair bit of experience hunting," he said. "Bobby is going to lead me into the woods after the tracks to see if we can get a sight of him and see what we're dealing with."

"It's definitely a bear?"

Bobby nodded. "It's a bit churned up out front," he said, "but you can see all of the tracks out back, clear as day. I was doing my rounds when I spotted them and knew they were heading toward the cabins. So I followed them and... found her."

"Did you know Marie DuVale?" she asked him, hearing a note of suspicion in her own voice. She saw Cooper glance at her sharply and she shrugged in response. Old habits die hard.

"I used to see her about," Bobby said. "She was friendly enough, but she was quiet too and never had much to say. She was always busy with her writing."

"Do you want to come with us, Price?" Cooper cut in, perhaps before Sadie could start interrogating Bobby as a potential "suspect."

Sadie hesitated. "Don't we need a proper team?"

"We're not going to try and take him out," Bobby said. "Just see if we can locate it and hopefully its lair. We'll hang back, stay downwind."

"I've called Game and Wildlife," Cooper said. "So we can get a proper hunt coordinated. But they can't get straight out here. The more information I've got, the better. As soon as this gets out, there's going to be a panic, or macho types taking the matter into their own hands. There are a lot of tourists and vacationers in these forest cabins. We don't want any more casualties."

"I could use some space to get all this catalogued," Pete cut in, obviously relishing the idea of getting them out of the way for a while. Sadie shrugged. *Why not? I don't have anything better to do,* she thought. She wasn't currently needed at the FBI field office in Anchorage. In fact, she wasn't due to return to work for a few more days, after her last case had seen her end up in the hospital.

Sadie would have happily gone straight back to work but Paul Golightly, her ASAC, had insisted she take some time out to recover.

Her plan had been to use it working on Jessica's cold case, but that had hit a dead end with her father lying in the hospital. The last thing she needed was to sit around worrying.

Even if she could think of more pleasant things to do than trek through freezing woods after a man-eating grizzly.

"Looks like we're going on a bear hunt, then," she said.

Before they left the cabin, she took a look back at the blood-spattered mess and realized that although the killer wasn't human this time, it was just as dangerous.

She hoped they weren't about to walk straight into its lair.

CHAPTER THREE

Sadie ducked, narrowly avoiding a heap of snow falling straight on her from the pines overhead. Instead, some of it hit her back and she let out an *oof* at the impact. Snow was heavier than it looked. Bobby Carson looked back at her with a frown at the noise and Sadie grimaced apologetically. The last thing they needed was to alert an angry bear to their presence.

As she followed Cooper and Carson, tiptoeing through the trees, she wondered if coming on this hunt had been a good idea. She knew no more about bears than the average Alaskan, and far from taking her mind away from her father's condition, she was finding herself assailed with memories.

Or at least, one memory in particular.

Most of the locals who lived out in the hinterlands liked to hunt, and her father had sometimes joined in on the bigger hunts, when a group of guys got together to take down a big grizzly like it was some kind of male bonding ritual. Some of them took their kids, but their mother had refused to let Jessica and Sadie go.

The year after her death, he had finally taken them on a bear hunt, and although Jessica had pulled a face and not wanted to go, Sadie had jumped at the chance to do something with her father. At that time, she had still wanted his approval, and when he had smiled at her eagerness to accompany him, she had basked in the attention. It was so rare that he looked at her with anything but disdain.

Jessica then had to come too, of course. The two girls were stuck by each other's side after their mother died.

Now, creeping through the pines after the sheriff and the trapper, Sadie remembered that other hunt, more than two decades ago. How she had held Jessica's hand, wide-eyed with excitement and more than a touch of fear. She had never seen a bear up close before, but she had heard stories of how they occasionally attacked humans and even made their way into people's homes if they scented food or blood, especially in winter when they were hungry.

The anticipation in the air had been palpable then, charged and focused, rather than the trepidation and caution with which the three of them moved through the forest now. She had a vivid auditory memory of the cry that had gone up when a big grizzly had lumbered out on the path ahead, roaring in outrage at the group of hunters.

But although Sadie knew they were there to kill the bear, she still hadn't been prepared for the actual event. She had watched through her father's legs as the creature—cartoonishly huge to a seven-year-old Sadie—had gone down, fighting and roaring until it took its last, shaky breath.

Then she had cried. The sight of the animal, which was as majestically beautiful to her as it was frightening, being senselessly killed just so some humans could have some fun, had shaken her to the core. It had just seemed so wrong.

Then her father had glared down at her with a searing look of disgust that still stung her even now.

He hadn't so much as looked at her for days after that, and the rejection had cut deep. Still, on reflection, his silence had been better than the beatings that came as she got older.

Sadie shook off the memory, feeling a cold that had nothing to do with the weather. This was the worst thing about coming back to Alaska—there were memories everywhere and they were rarely good ones.

She took a deep breath, inhaling the frosty air so that it chilled her lungs, and brought herself back to the present, surveying the landscape around her. They were coming through the trees now, out onto desolate tundra. She could hear running water and knew they were approaching the headwaters of the river that ran out of the mountains and filled most of the frozen lakes in the Lynx Lake Loop, a web of pools that were popular with the ice fishermen.

Up ahead, Carson stopped, shaking his head. "I've lost the trail," he said. "But if we head toward the river—good hunting ground for salmon at this time of year—then we might be able to pick it up again."

They carried on through deepening snow until the tundra fell away in a steep drop to the river below. They were practically on a cliff edge, looking down into an icy valley. Although further toward civilization the water would be frozen, here it was still bubbling out of the earth, a sparkle of movement in the frosty stillness all around.

But the river wasn't the only thing they were looking down at. Hearing both Carson and the sheriff gasp, Sadie peered over the gorge and her eyes went wide at the sight below her.

There was not just one grizzly at the headwaters of the river, happily hunting for salmon, but a dozen, a few of them youngsters.

15

The three of them stepped back from the edge and stared at each other incredulously.

"Well," the sheriff said eventually, sounding stunned. "That wasn't what I was expecting."

Carson shook his head. "We're gon' need a big ol' hunt to get our killer...or killers."

Sadie frowned at him. "You can't just kill all of them and hope you get the right one. Besides, there are mothers with young there too, and they're illegal to hunt."

Carson looked disappointed, and Sadie suspected that he had been having visions of twelve stuffed bear heads neatly lined up on his cabin wall. She looked at Cooper, who was already taking his radio out of his pocket while still blinking in disbelief. Sadie almost felt sorry for him. Less than a month after a brutal murder case, he now had not just one but potentially twelve dangerous grizzlies on his hands.

"I need to speak to Game and Wildlife again," he said. "And get an expert out here who knows what the hell to do in this situation. There are rules about hunting bears, I can't just set up a local hunt. Ideally, we need to identify and isolate the animal we're looking for."

"Will that even be possible?" Sadie asked, looking down at the grizzlies again and, just as she had as a child, thinking how beautiful they were.

"That's why we need an expert," Cooper said. He radioed through and spoke to someone who assured him they would get someone out right away. Then he put his radio back inside his coat and joined Sadie at the edge, looking down at the bears.

"You weren't expecting this," Sadie said. Cooper whistled through his teeth.

"No, I wasn't. I just hope this guy that they're sending knows his stuff. We need to get a handle on this."

"What if," Sadie ventured hesitantly, "there was more than one of them? Or a few of them get a taste for human flesh?"

Cooper stared down into the gorge, his expression darkening.

"Then we're all in big trouble," he said.

CHAPTER FOUR

Sadie couldn't stop staring at the bears. At their sleek winter coats and the powerful slide of the muscles underneath their skin. Even the adolescent bears looked as though they could easily rip any one of them apart.

She thought of what Marie's final moments must have been like and shuddered. It was no way to go.

But then, was wasting away ravaged by cancer, as her father had been doing, really any kinder? Marie's death must have been quick at least. The bears looked as though they wouldn't have wasted any time. Even though they were way above the animals, looking down over the headwaters, Sadie felt a shiver of fear as she watched the largest of them raise its head and sniff the air.

"Can it smell us?" she said to no one in particular. Carson shook his head.

"Wouldn't have thought so. Wind is in the wrong direction. Why?" he asked, almost leering at her as though he found the idea amusing. "Are you scared?"

Sadie eyeballed him hard.

"Considering one of them just ripped Ms. DuVale to death, caution might be a good idea," she snapped. Carson shrugged amiably and turned away. Sadie watched him for a few moments, still unable to shake her initial suspicion, before she turned back to the bears.

Behind them an engine rumbled. A battered old Ford Bronco came into view and stopped, and a man who looked to be in his mid-thirties stepped out.

Suddenly Sadie had something else to look at other than bears.

He was naturally tanned and dark-eyed, which clashed with what appeared to be naturally blond hair, although not in an unpleasant way. Under his parka and jeans, he was clearly buff, and there was a no-nonsense appearance to him that belied his movie star looks.

Sadie realized the sheriff was watching her and knew that she was staring, but it was difficult not to. The guy could have stepped off a movie set.

"And you are?" Sheriff Cooper asked, sounding less than pleased.

"Game and Wildlife sent me," the man said, holding his hand out and smiling as though he hadn't even noticed Cooper's tone. He had full lips and white, even teeth. Sadie felt uncharacteristically self-conscious of her messy hair and unmade-up face. "I'm Rick Bonsor, zoologist. I specialize in bear attacks. I was told you had a nasty one?"

"We do," Sadie said, cutting in before Cooper had the chance to reply. She gave him the swift lowdown on Marie's body. "Mr. Carson here is a local tracker. We came out to have a look and, well, this is what we found." She motioned him toward the edge of the gorge, ignoring Cooper's baleful glare. This was his jurisdiction, after all, and she was taking over.

Rick looked down at the bears and gave a sharp inhale as he watched them through narrowed eyes.

"Is there any way of working out which one we need to take down?" Cooper asked, shooting a look at Sadie as though telling her to leave this to him. Rick nodded.

"Potentially. As I'm sure you know, attacks of this nature are pretty rare. Mostly bears just want to be left alone and will only attack if threatened or, of course, hungry. Bears will sniff around cabins but usually out of curiosity than aggression. However, they are opportunists. If our guy was starving and came across Marie…it may well have been too tempting to leave alone."

"So it's likely to be a one-off?" Sadie said, surprised at how interested she was in the subject. It didn't hurt when it was being delivered by a guy this handsome, she thought wryly to herself. Her last relationship had been a long time ago and while Sadie was hardly the eyelash-fluttering type, she wasn't immune to an attractive man either.

"I would hope so. Unfortunately, if a bear gets a taste for human flesh, it could come back for more. They are an apex predator. Without technology, we don't stand a chance against them. You will need to raise the alarm to any locals. Potentially evacuate the area if we don't find him or her fast."

Cooper rubbed his chin, looking perturbed.

"We'll need to handle this carefully; we don't want to cause a panic," he said. "The sooner we can get a hunt set up, the better."

Sadie saw a flash of annoyance cross Rick's face. "We need to know which bear we're looking for first, Sheriff," he said, his voice harder than it had been before Cooper's comment. "I don't want to see innocent animals gunned down for no reason. There are cubs down there. Enough bear populations are threatened by hunters as it is."

Cooper's jaw set stubbornly, an expression Sadie recognized all too well. "Maybe, Mr. Bonsor," he said stiffly. "But I don't want to see innocent citizens torn apart by feral animals on my watch either. Perhaps you can get on with locating our culprit?"

The zoologist bristled visibly, and Sadie could feel the tenson crackling in the air between the two men as they stared at each other, shoulders back and jaws jutting. You could almost taste the testosterone in the air.

"When you two have finished your pissing contest," she said, hearing Carson snicker behind her, "perhaps we can all get on with our jobs? Maybe we should go back to the cabin, Sheriff, and take another look around? Check we're not missing anything?"

Cooper looked at her, his eyebrows raised, and for a moment Sadie thought he was going to say something about how he was the one in charge here, but instead he nodded tersely.

"Let's do that, Price. Mr. Bonsor, if you could report back as soon as you have any information?"

Rick was looking down at the bears again, and the crackling tension had dissipated. *Men,* Sadie thought, shaking her head.

"Sure. It might take a while. I need to observe their behavior, their different personality types. These 'feral' animals are actually highly intelligent beings, Sheriff."

"Yeah. Some killers are," Cooper responded before walking off. Sadie followed, resisting a glance back at Rick Bonsor, although she was sure she could feel the handsome zoologist's eyes on her.

*

"What was all that about?" Sadie asked in a low voice as they approached the cabin. Carson was still lingering around behind them. Sadie was surprised Cooper hadn't told him they no longer needed him, but the sheriff seemed preoccupied. She couldn't help wondering if it was because of Rick, and how she felt about the possibility that Cooper was only threatened by the other man because of her presence.

It wouldn't be the first time Cooper had seemed jealous of other men sniffing around her, even if Sadie knew that he would rather face down a bear single-handedly than admit it.

Not that Rick had been sniffing around, she reprimanded herself. If anything, it had been she who could barely stop drooling. Not very professional, letting herself get distracted by a handsome face.

Right now, though, a distraction could be just what she needed.

"I didn't like him," Cooper said. "He seems arrogant. I've met his type before. Thinks he knows everything; he could hold up the hunt."

Sadie decided not to pursue the conversation. As they walked through the front garden of the cabin, she had other things on her mind again. Bits of food were scattered along the path; the leftovers of the grizzly's starter before his main course of Marie DuVale.

"It's almost like a trail," she thought out loud, and then stopped dead on the path.

"Carson," she called back to the trapper, "would Ms. DuVale have known about the relevant bear mitigation measures and how to keep herself safe?"

"Sure," the trapper responded. "Everyone who stays here does, and Game and Wildlife sends out resources."

Sadie motioned for Cooper to follow her inside, and she shut the cabin door to prevent Carson following them further. Pete was still there, and the place was as gory and smelly as before, but Sadie was now looking at it differently.

She was looking at it as though it was a crime scene.

"What's wrong, Price?" Cooper asked with a frown. Sadie waved her hand around the kitchen.

"Look at all the food that was left out, well within reach," she said. "Add that to the scraps left in the front garden, and it's almost as though someone left a trail of breadcrumbs for the bear to follow. Leading it right to Marie."

The sheriff looked at her as though she had lost her mind.

"Price," he said slowly, lowering his tone so the medical examiner couldn't hear, "not everything is some crazed serial killer. I know we've had a few awful cases lately, but...come on. This is a bear attack."

Sadie looked around, wondering if the sheriff was right. She had spent so much of her life hunting killers that she was starting to see them everywhere. She ran a hand over her scalp, messing her hair up further. Cooper's expression softened as he watched her.

"Are you okay?" he asked. "How did it go with your father?"

Sadie swallowed, fighting the sudden threat of tears. She didn't want to talk about her father, not yet. She didn't even want to think about him.

"Not good," she admitted. "He's in the hospital. He had a heart attack before he could tell me anything. He was about to though, I'm sure of it."

Cooper looked stunned. "What the hell? Why didn't you say something? I wouldn't have dragged you out here if I had known. You need to be with him."

Sadie sighed heavily and collected herself, regaining her composure. If there was one emotion she couldn't handle from other people, it was pity.

"He's in a coma, he wouldn't even know I was there. And honestly, he wouldn't want me there if he was awake. The hospital will phone me right away if there's any change. And I'm glad you called me," she admitted. "I'm better off keeping busy than sitting around thinking about it all. I can't do anything about it, so I may as well do something useful."

"You need to go home and rest," Cooper said, sounding exasperated with her. "Go on, I'll call you tomorrow."

Knowing that it was pointless arguing and that there was nothing more that she could do there in any case, Sadie nodded.

"Okay," she said, turning to go. She looked back over her shoulder at the sheriff, almost desperately. "Just...keep me in the loop, okay?"

"Sure," he said, and she cringed at the look of sympathy in his eyes. She knew he thought her theory was completely crazy.

She shut the cabin door behind her, relieved to see that Carson had disappeared. As she climbed into her truck, something caught her eye.

There was a Jeep parked among the trees, partially hidden by the foliage, but not so hidden that Sadie didn't catch a glimpse of the driver. It looked like a man, with field glasses over his eyes.

They were focused on the cabin.

Sadie looked casually away, taking her time turning on the heat inside her truck and getting herself strapped in. From the corner of her eye, she saw the truck start to pull away.

After a few moments, she followed.

CHAPTER FIVE

The Jeep, now that they were out of the woods and on the back roads heading toward Anchorage, was a cut above the battered vehicles that Sadie was used to seeing around the hinterlands. It was a new model, a black stretch that must have cost more than most of the locals' houses.

It was a detail that pricked her curiosity even further. She hung back, keeping the Jeep just within her sights as they started to approach the main road into the outskirts of Anchorage. She wondered if the driver lived in the nicer suburbs, but he seemed to be heading more toward the port.

Named aptly as a place for vessels to anchor, the small city was a harbor town that had been founded in 1914 at the base of the glacial Chugach Mountains, intended as a base for the Alaska railroad.

Sadie had once heard Anchorage described as the state's "cultural soul" due to its tendency to attract artists and musicians, but growing up, that hadn't been the side of it she had seen. Living outside of town in the hinterlands in her father's cabin, she had only traveled into Anchorage—weather allowing—for school, occasional visits to the doctor, and shopping. Jessica had loved the mall, whereas Sadie had been happier hanging out at the frozen lakes or up in the pine woods.

She and her friends had been lucky, she mused, that they had never bumped into a hungry grizzly.

In the years that she had been gone, Anchorage had continued to thrive as a major city and commercial center in Alaska and was a major spot for tourists. But like most cities, it had its underbelly, and that included one of the highest crime rates of any city in America.

When Sadie had first returned, she had expected it to be quiet, even boring. It had been anything but.

As the Jeep in front of her turned onto a side road, Sadie realized where it was headed: Anchorage Business Park, an industrial estate that was home to fourteen commercial buildings with shiny steel and glass exteriors, punctuated by neat tree-lined verges. With the ground covered in snow, the winter sun sparkled off the windows as Sadie turned into the park, being careful to hang back from the Jeep.

Perhaps too careful. *Damn it, I lost him,* she thought as she drove slowly through the park, looking for the Jeep. She located it outside a four-story high rise, in a private parking bay. Sadie pulled over and looked at the signs on the outside of the building, sucking in her breath as she saw just where she was.

Clarity Land Development was a big-time land development company, which was often unpopular with more traditional locals and natives, especially out in the hinterlands. The company regularly bought up land for new roads and utilities and sold it on for major profit. Not so long ago, Sadie had heard regulars in Caz's Saloon joke that George McAllister, the CEO of Clarity, would sell the Chugach Mountains themselves if he could.

She was beginning to understand who owned that Jeep—but not why McAllister would be spying on a recent bear attack in the woods.

Did Clarity have an interest in the area? A band of roaming grizzlies could certainly be a barrier to any new developments that they were planning.

Sadie undid her long, wavy hair and tied it back into a neater bun, straightened her clothes, and, making sure her badge was visible, got out of her truck, striding purposefully toward the entrance of Clarity Land Development.

The lobby was as fancy as she was expecting, with a large marble reception, plush cream carpets, and softly painted walls. Miniature models and concept art of upcoming developments were everywhere, and an immaculately made-up blonde receptionist greeted visitors with a megawatt smile. Feeling distinctly scruffy, Sadie went over to her and smiled politely.

The woman flashed what looked to be incredibly expensive veneers. Clearly working at Clarity paid very well. *I'm in the wrong job,* Sadie thought wryly, trying not to feel self-conscious about her muddy snow boots.

"Can I help you, ma'am?" the receptionist asked. Then her eyes fell on Sadie's badge and her plucked eyebrows shot up her forehead. The smile dimmed somewhat.

"I'd like to speak with Mr. McAllister, please," she said. The woman hesitated.

"Um, I'll check if he's here."

"Oh?" Sadie said innocently, checking out her hunch. "Didn't I just see him come in? He parked his Jeep outside, right?"

The receptionist looked flustered. "Yes, but I think he went straight into a meeting. Wait just one second and I'll call Mr. McAllister's secretary." She stood up and walked across the reception to use a phone, even though there was another right in front of her. After a brief conversation, she came back over with a small business card.

"Here's his secretary's number," she said pleasantly. "If you would like to call her you can arrange an appointment with Mr. McAllister."

Sadie looked at the card in the woman's hand. "I just need to ask a few questions," she pressed. The receptionist, having regained her composure, shrugged nonchalantly.

"If you call his secretary, you can make an appointment," she echoed. Sadie sighed impatiently.

"It would be easier if I could just make one now, while I'm here."

The receptionist looked at her blankly and handed her the card. Sadie took it and walked off, feeling annoyed at the way she had been brushed off, but knowing that she had no justifiable reason to demand that the man talk to her.

As she walked toward the exit, a land survey on the wall caught her attention. Holding her breath, she went closer, taking in the details of the survey.

It was a map of the outlying areas, the places she knew as the hinterlands, or the backwoods. Scattered cabins and lakes in the shadows of the Chugach, home to hunters and trappers, ice fishermen, and loners like her father.

It also encompassed the more up-market cabins where Marie DuVale had lived. In fact, as Sadie peered closer, her heart began to beat more rapidly as she saw exactly which area was highlighted in bright pink and was under planning to become a five-star resort. She shook her head, realizing just how little had been reported about this in the local press. A resort of this size, while no doubt bringing in plenty of jobs and tourism, was also likely to involve a lot of wildlife destruction and the buying out of people's homes.

More importantly, however, was the fact that Marie DuVale's cabin was right in the center of the highlighted area.

What are the odds?

Sadie turned on her heel and walked swiftly out of the building, calling Cooper as she climbed back into her truck. The sheriff answered on the second ring, sounding worried.

"Price? How are things with your father?"

"It's not about that," she said swiftly, and explained about seeing the Jeep and following it back to the Clarity building. "It was George McAllister himself," she said excitedly, "watching Marie's cabin through field glasses."

There was a long pause. "Are you sure about this, Price?" Cooper asked, sounding dubious.

"Of course," Sadie said impatiently. "I've just checked with the receptionist. And discovered exactly why he may have been watching the area."

"Go on." Cooper sounded wary. Sadie explained about the land survey on the wall, and the plans for the five-star resort.

"Marie's cabin is right in the middle of the planned resort area. The development wouldn't be able to go ahead without her agreeing to sell to them. Perhaps she refused."

Sadie was expecting Cooper to find this latest info as suspicious as she did, but Cooper just sounded puzzled. "Sadie, what are you talking about?"

Sadie felt her face burning, suddenly feeling foolish. "It means there's a motive... Come on, Cooper, you said yourself that the food at the cabin looked like a trail."

"So, what you are telling me," the sheriff said, sounding as though he couldn't believe his ears, "is that George McAllister set a trail of food to lure a grizzly bear to Marie's cabin in the hope that it would eat her, all because she wouldn't sell her cabin to them?"

Put like that, Sadie had to admit that it sounded fantastical. She slumped in her seat, rubbing a hand over her eyes. She was tired and they were stinging. The need for rest was overwhelming as the adrenaline from following McAllister subsided, leaving her feeling scrubbed out and raw. Even so, she attempted to defend her theory.

"The resort will bring in millions of dollars for Clarity, if not billions. Money has always been a prime motive."

Cooper gave an exasperated sigh. "Price, listen to me," he said firmly. "We are not looking for a motive. There is no murder and no evidence of one. This was a bear attack. You can't go throwing ludicrous theories around just because of a survey on a wall and him being near the scene. He could have been goddamn birdwatching for all we know."

Sadie felt stung by his dismissal. Okay, she conceded to herself, it was a little far-fetched, but she had been right before when Cooper had been adamant that she was wrong, and in her experience, when too many little coincidences started to add up, it usually meant that they were not in fact coincidences at all.

"Fine," she snapped, "that's your opinion on it. I still think it's worth questioning him; I'm going to make an appointment with his secretary."

"You are not," Cooper argued. "Just go home, Price, and let it go, will you?"

Sadie bristled at his trying to order her around. "You can't tell me what to do, Sheriff. I'm a federal agent. I'm going to question McAllister."

Cooper muttered something under his breath and Sadie suspected it wasn't words of endearment.

"Do what you want, Price," he sighed, "but it's nothing to do with me, like you say. So don't complain to me when Golightly comes down hard on you for this."

"Why would he?"

"Because McAllister has big-time political juice in this town, and you can bet your bottom dollar he will kick up one hell of a stink if FBI agents start harassing him over being in the wrong place at the wrong time. Especially when there isn't even an open investigation. This will be ruled as a bear attack because that's what it is. If you want to go rogue, that's up to you." Cooper hesitated, and when Sadie didn't reply he said more softly, "Price, you've had quite an ordeal today. Don't rip my head off, but maybe you're a bit...overwrought."

Sadie had to bite her lip to prevent herself from hollering and cussing down the phone at him.

Especially when common sense told her that he was right.

"Fine," she snapped again. "I'll see you around." She hung up, started the truck, and drove off quickly, resentment and frustration burning in her gut.

As she drove, she called the hospital to check on her father even though she knew she would have been contacted if there was any update.

Sure enough, the nurse told her that there was no change in his condition. Sadie turned on the radio, trying to drown out her thoughts.

She turned it back off when the evening news informed her of the bear attack that had killed local author Marie DuVale.

She needed a drink.

CHAPTER SIX

As she entered the saloon, Caz, the owner, looked up from behind the bar and smiled warmly at her. As weary as she felt, Sadie returned the smile.

Since her return, she had become fast friends with Caz, the butch-looking bartender with a heart of gold. Caz was a single mother to a little girl named Jenny who absolutely adored Sadie.

"Soft drink or a stiff one?" Caz asked, taking in Sadie's expression. Sadie had been on orange juice recently as she had been recovering from her hospital stay, but after the events of today, an OJ just wasn't going to cut it.

"Whiskey, please," Sadie ordered. "A double," she added. Caz fetched her the drink without questioning her.

"Where's Jenny?" Sadie asked. Ever since Caz's au pair had gone back to Paraguay, Sadie knew that she had been having trouble juggling looking after Jenny with tending the bar. Caz was popular, however, and a few of the local women had stepped in to help, as well as her cousin Ron, who also helped out behind the bar.

"Upstairs, watching TV," Caz said with a sigh. "Ron will cover the bar for me later so I can get her to bed. I'm going to have to give him those extra hours; he's been asking for months anyway, but it's going to be tight."

Sadie nodded sympathetically. While the saloon always had customers, it was a steady trickle rather than a crowd, and she knew that Caz often struggled to make ends meet as a single parent. She perched on her usual barstool, ignoring the curious looks of the other regulars at the bar, mostly old boys who knew her father.

She usually tried to avoid speaking to them, because sooner or later someone always brought up either her father's illness or her sister's death. The last thing she needed was to have to relay her father's cardiac arrest to his old friends and acquaintances. None of them had visited him for years, even once his cancer had become common knowledge.

"Have you heard about the bear attack?" Caz said as she set Sadie's drink down in front of her. "I just heard it on the radio."

Sadie nodded. "I was just at the scene with the sheriff." She decided not to tell Caz about the group of bears they had seen, not while there were so many eager ears around. It would cause a panic and, no doubt, an impromptu hunt that could well end up being illegal.

"Oh? Not your usual work," Caz said, looking curious. Sadie just shrugged. She could fill her friend in on the details later. Right now, she just needed to relax and stop thinking about it all.

The reprimand from the sheriff had left her feeling humiliated, but she still couldn't shake the feeling that something was wrong with the whole case. Whatever Cooper said, McAllister's presence near the cabin was suspicious, and it warranted questioning him about it.

She just had to hope that Golightly agreed, or she was likely to get seriously chewed out by her boss for offending local public figures. It wouldn't be the first time Sadie had stepped on the wrong toes.

"Well, will you look at that," Caz said in a muffled voice, her eyes fixed on the entrance to the saloon. Recognizing the tone in Caz's voice that meant she had spotted an attractive man, Sadie followed the bartender's gaze in amusement, wondering who her latest prey was.

She felt her cheeks flame as she saw that it was Rick Bonsor. In the low, smoky light of the saloon his good looks were even more striking, and Sadie felt her stomach flip in a way it hadn't since she had been a schoolgirl with a crush.

Rick spotted Sadie and grinned, heading straight for the stool next to her. "Agent Price," he said, sounding more than pleased to see her. "Or should I call you something else now that you're off duty?"

"It's Sadie," she said, aiming for nonchalance only to wince when her voice came out higher than usual. She could feel Caz's eyes burning into her and tried to ignore them, taking a too large sip of her whiskey that made her cough. Caz leaned over the bar and banged Sadie loudly on the back.

"Easy, girl. When you've finished choking, perhaps you could introduce me?"

"I'm Rick," the zoologist said, sounding amused. "I'm here to investigate the bear attack that occurred this morning. And right now, I'd like a beer."

"Coming right up," Caz said with a wink that was anything but subtle. As she went to fetch the beer, Sadie shifted awkwardly in her seat, trying to think of something to say. *This is ridiculous,* she told herself sternly. *It's not as though you have never seen a man before.*

"Did you discover much about our resident grizzlies?" she asked eventually, keeping her voice low. Rick got the message, leaning in close to her to answer. Their knees were nearly touching, and Sadie felt her heart rate speed up ever so slightly.

"I've done some preliminary work on the bear population," he said. "There's one big boy in particular who seems more aggressive than the others, and fearless, so I may have found our culprit, but it's too early to say. Of course, the only way to be certain is to actually catch him in the act, but that's hardly desirable."

"Do they usually gather in groups like that? I always thought bears were solitary."

"Generally, they are," he agreed. "But they will congregate at certain times. A river full of salmon is one of them. It's a rich food source for them and right now they are hungry as hell. It's quite something, to see a group of them all together like this." His eyes shone and Sadie could see how passionate he was about his subject. It only made him look more attractive. She had respect for that level of drive.

"Well, one of them thought the salmon was only a starter," said a dry voice behind them that made Sadie startle. She turned in her seat to see Sheriff Cooper eyeing the virtually non-existent space between Rick and Sadie and looking less than impressed by it. He smiled stiffly at Sadie, barely acknowledging Rick as the man nodded at him in greeting.

It seemed that the sheriff really didn't like their new bear expert.

Or at least, he didn't seem to like him being around Sadie.

The thought was there before she could quash it. The sheriff was jealous. And as much as Sadie was determined that work and romance should never, ever mix, she couldn't deny that the idea of the sheriff being jealous over her wasn't totally unpleasant.

On their last case together there had been a few fleeting moments when Sadie had felt the spark of something between them, but she was scared of letting that spark catch fire. Cooper was a colleague and had also become a friend, one who had agreed to open up a cold case on Jessica's death and investigate it with her. She valued their working relationship and had no intention of screwing it up for a fling. Sheriff Cooper was a no-go area.

Rick Bonsor, though, could be pure, unadulterated fun…if Sadie could just let herself go for five minutes. Caz wouldn't think twice, and Sadie admired the easy confidence of the other woman.

Perhaps, for once, things didn't have to be so complicated.

Except now the sheriff had turned up, and complicated was exactly how she felt.

"Cooper," Sadie murmured, not meeting his eyes.

29

Caz was back at the bar, handing Rick his beer with her eyes firmly on the sheriff. She had a longstanding crush on Logan Cooper that Sadie was pretty sure the whole of Anchorage was aware of.

"Nice to see you, Logan. You're not often here off duty, what can I get you?"

"My usual," Cooper said. "But I don't want to break up the party," he sniped, glancing pointedly at Sadie and Rick. Rick just looked amused, and Sadie guessed he was probably all too used to this reaction from other men. He must be aware of the way he looked and the effect that he had on women.

"I don't think anyone feels much like partying after today," Sadie said coolly. Cooper shrugged and leaned on the bar next to Rick, taking his bottle of beer from Caz, who was eyeing them all astutely. The bar owner looked at Sadie with raised eyebrows and Sadie stifled a groan, knowing her friend would want a full rundown of the situation later.

"When do you think you can get this investigate wrapped up, Bonsor?" the sheriff asked, barely bothering to sound polite. Rick's expression changed from amiable to annoyed.

"It isn't something that can be rushed, Sheriff," he protested. "This needs careful handling. The bear population has been dwindling around here, so I'm glad to see such a group. We want to avoid hunting the wrong animal."

Cooper looked outraged. "I'm more concerned about people than bears," he said. "And as much as I don't want to kill innocent animals, I would rather see a few dead bears than any more locals ripped to shreds by a rogue beast. My job is to protect citizens, Bonsor, not go all warm and fuzzy over wild animals."

The two men glared at each other just as they had earlier, and Sadie suppressed a sigh. *Here we go again,* she thought. Two alpha males trying to outdo each other.

"Those wild animals are some of Alaska's most magnificent creatures," Rick snapped. "I appreciate your concern, Sheriff, and I will do all I can to solve this problem for you, but it is still part of my job to protect the bears that aren't responsible for the poor woman's death."

"The locals will start hunting them anyway," Caz cut in, "once they get wind that there's a bunch of grizzlies around. Apart from any moms and cubs, of course. Bear hunting is popular around here when folks get the chance."

Rick shook his head in disgust. As a zoologist, he wouldn't approve of hunting for sport, Sadie guessed. Although brown grizzlies weren't an endangered species, they were afforded some protections and as a mascot for the state they were beloved by a lot of the citizens. Hunts had been protested before.

"I can tell you're not local," Cooper said to Rick, the tone of his voice implying that this was some kind of slur.

"Why, do only true Alaskans love hunting and trapping, Sheriff?" Rick asked almost mockingly. "We're not all living in the Dark Ages. Conservation and diversity of wildlife is important. We need apex predators, they're a vital part of ecological systems."

"Not when they start munching down on locals under my jurisdiction, they're not," Cooper growled, sounding not un-bearlike himself. Sadie didn't think she had ever seen him so riled. Rick Bonsor had really gotten under his skin.

She wasn't going to let herself think too hard about the possible reasons why. She finished her drink and set her glass down on the counter.

"I'll leave you guys to your ongoing pissing contest," she said, invoking a snort of laughter from Caz. "I'm going home." She slid off her stool.

"I'll see you there," Caz called after her, grinning.

Sadie didn't look back at either the sheriff or Rick as she walked away, but she could feel their eyes on her as she left.

CHAPTER SEVEN

For the past few weeks, "home" for Sadie had been a fleabag motel on the wrong side of town, not that she had spent much time there. Her reintroduction to Alaska had been rougher than she had expected.

It had been her plan, once things had calmed down, to rent a small apartment in Anchorage, close to the FBI field office. Fate, however, had other plans.

Now she lived with Caz and Jenny in the room vacated by the last au pair. It wasn't supposed to be anything other than another temporary arrangement, but now Caz was talking about cleaning out the room above her garage and leasing that to her. It would make a cozy little studio apartment, and Sadie was more than tempted.

Not least because, in a short space of time, Caz and Jenny were beginning to feel like family.

Before she went to her room to get a much-needed early night, she poked her head into the small apartment to say goodnight to Jenny, who was sitting in front of *Rick and Morty* with a tub of ice cream. Ron, Caz's younger cousin and part-time bartender, lay on the sofa laughing at the cartoon.

"Should she be watching that?" Sadie asked, sure that it wasn't written for younger kids, but Ron shrugged, and Jenny jumped up and ran over to give her a hug. Sadie forgot about the cartoon as she kissed the top of the little girl's blonde head. An instant pang of grief overwhelmed her, but she wasn't sure if the feeling was for Jessica, their father, or herself. For the little girl she had once been who had longed for a proper family home just like this.

"Goodnight, sweetie," she murmured and then turned away before tears threatened. Her mood was mercurial today, a sure sign that the stress was getting to her.

As she collapsed onto the small, slightly too hard mattress in what was now her room, she prayed that her usual nightmares wouldn't come, and was grateful when she fell into an all-enveloping, inky blackness.

*

"I couldn't sleep." Sadie joined Caz by the firepit at the back porch, where Caz was smoking and looking up at the stars in front of a smoldering firepit. It was past midnight now and this was often a nightly ritual of Caz's, to sneak out of the bedroom she shared with her daughter and have a solitary smoke by a homemade fire. Sometimes, like tonight, Sadie joined her.

"I got an hour or so, then woke up and couldn't get back to sleep," she continued as she squatted down next to Caz, stretching out her hands to warm them next to the fire. Caz glanced over at her and took a long drag on her cigarette.

"You got things on your mind?"

Sadie tipped her head back, looking up at the scattered stars, which seemed closer than usual in the winter sky, burning with a cold light that illuminated the snow and ice all around her. The Alaska landscape was as beautiful as it was deadly, she thought, wondering what was lurking out in the woods tonight. Hungry bears...or worse?

"You could say that. My father was admitted to hospital today. Cardiac arrest."

Caz's eyes widened. "And you're only just telling me now? How is he?"

"In a coma," Sadie said, feeling oddly detached from the subject, as though she was relaying information about someone else's family. The events of the morning felt surreal, overshadowed by the bear attack and her suspicions of McAllister. She suspected that Cooper knew her better than she would like to admit, and those suspicions were at least partly driven by a desire to avoid thinking about her father's predicament.

Although she didn't usually smoke, Sadie took the cigarette that Caz offered her and took a drag of it. The harsh burn of the tobacco at the back of her throat was almost a relief.

"Are you going to see him?" Caz asked tentatively. Sadie had confided in her recently about her past with her father, and about Jessica. Hell, most of Anchorage knew about Jessica, although not that Sadie was reopening the case on her own time.

"I was there when it happened," Sadie said, wincing at the memory of the pain and fear that had suddenly twisted her father's expression. Caz looked shocked.

"Damn, hon, you should have told me. And you just went straight back out to work?"

"It wasn't even really work," Sadie admitted. "I was just tagging along to give myself something to do. You know me, Caz, I like to get on with things. No point dwelling on what I can't change."

"Oh, you're a tough cookie, I know that," Caz said sagely, flicking ash into the fire, "but sometimes if you don't bend, you break. Life hasn't exactly gone easy on you since you returned, has it?"

Sadie shrugged, not sure what to say to that. She couldn't think of a time when life had ever been particularly easy.

"I didn't expect it to, but yeah, this morning was a shock. I know he's ill, and probably hasn't got much time left anyway, but it was so sudden. One minute he was talking—well, shouting, to be exact—then he keeled over." Sadie shook her head as she remembered how fragile he had looked in the hospital bed. "I'm not sure he will wake up from this, to be honest. I've spoken to the hospital and there's been no change since he was admitted."

Caz was quiet for a while, but just the presence of the other woman was comforting. As different as they were in many respects, Caz was rapidly becoming her closest friend. The Coopers too—both the sheriff and his sister Jane, who was the local deputy—were becoming important fixtures in her life. While she was glad that she had supportive people in her life, there were times when it unnerved her. She had lived her entire life putting barriers between herself and anyone who attempted to get too close. Having learned loss at an early age, she had no wish to experience it again.

"I'll go and see him tomorrow," Sadie said into the silence. "Although if I'm honest with myself, I don't know if I really even want to." She hesitated, surprised at her own words. "Does that make me a terrible person?" she asked, a slight wobble in her voice.

"Not at all," Caz said firmly. "There's a reason you don't see my family around here. Sometimes we've just gotta stay away from people, whether they're blood or not. The way he treated you, you've got nothing to feel bad about."

Sadie wished she felt as certain of that as Caz seemed to. She suppressed a yawn, feeling a fresh wave of fatigue coming over her. She should go back to bed, but for a moment she felt acutely the need to not be alone right now.

"I can sense you don't wanna talk about him," Caz said. "Just know I'm here if you need a shoulder, okay?"

"I know," Sadie said, giving her a genuine if weak smile.

Then Caz grinned. "On a lighter note," she said, and Sadie knew exactly what subject the barkeeper was about to turn to, "just how gorgeous is that animal guy?"

Sadie laughed, her worries momentarily forgotten. She had known that Rick Bonsor's good looks would not escape Caz's notice.

"He is easy on the eye," she admitted. "Cooper doesn't seem too keen though."

"Of course he doesn't," Caz said. "Logan Cooper is too used to being the local heartthrob and claiming all the female attention, as much as he pretends not to notice it. And we all know he has a soft spot for you."

"He's just a…"

"Work colleague. I know." Caz finished her sentence for her. The relationship—or lack of—between Sadie and Cooper was one that had come up on a number of occasions, always instigated by Caz herself.

Sadie shook her head. "It's silly. Rick is just here to help with catching the bear. Then he'll be gone."

"No harm in a little fling in the meantime. He was eyeing you like he'd never seen a woman before."

"I only met him today," Sadie said, trying not to react but wondering if Caz was right. Her friend grinned knowingly.

"You like him too, then."

Sadie waved a hand dismissively, although she was glad it was dark enough that the other woman couldn't entirely read her expression. Caz could be too astute for her own good.

"I'm not immune to a good-looking guy, Caz. But I don't have time for a 'little fling.' I doubt I will see him again anyway. I'm back to work at the field office this week. The bear hunt isn't part of my job description. Cooper and Rick can puff their chests out at each other as much as they like; I won't be around to see it."

As she spoke, she realized that she would miss working side by side with the Coopers every day. But without a local murder case to work on, Golightly would need her elsewhere.

Of course, there was Jessica's case, which Cooper had agreed to help her with, but she didn't want to think about that now. If her father never woke up, then the investigation would be over before it had begun.

And she would never know what had happened to her sister.

Sadie stood up. She was freezing now and ready for sleep again. Or at least her body was. Her head whirled with thoughts of her father, Jessica, and poor Marie DuVale and the group of bears at the river head. She said goodnight to Caz and went back up to bed, hoping that sleep would bring some relief.

She wondered what fresh horrors the morning would bring.

CHAPTER EIGHT

Sadie followed her father through the pine woods, pulling her too large parka tightly around herself against the bitter wind. It howled loudly in her ears, and she wondered if there were wolves out there, hiding up in the mountains.

Only it wasn't a wolf they were tracking, but a bear.

This time, Jessica wasn't with them. Sadie was vaguely aware that this was unusual, because Jessica was always with her, especially when their father was around, shielding Sadie from his explosive and often unexpected anger.

Yet tonight, it was just Sadie and her dad, and he seemed as scared as she was.

She could see her breath curling in the air in front of her, and there was frost on her eyelashes. The trees reared above her, black and spiky against a moonlit sky. The landscape that looked so austerely beautiful in the daylight was the backdrop to a horror movie at night, with shadows that looked so deep they could be hiding monsters from the depths of hell.

"How much further, Dad?" Sadie asked, her voice a whisper. He hissed at her sharply, warning her to keep quiet.

"We've got his tracks," he murmured, his voice alert for once and not slurred with drink as it was most nights. "Look."

Sadie looked at the frozen ground in front of them and saw them in the light of her father's flash; pawprints that stretched ahead into the distance, taking them right into the dark heart of the woods. They were huge. Far too large for a bear. She wanted to beg her father to turn back, to pull at his coat to stop him going forward, but she knew what the likely response would be and so she continued to follow.

But where was Jessica?

As they continued to creep through the trees, she saw the pawprints getting larger and deeper, and terror filled her at the thought of confronting the creature that had made those marks.

Then she saw liquid gleaming in the indentations in the snow left by the monster's feet.

"What's that, Dad? In the prints?" Her voice trembled as her father leaned down to see.

"It's blood," he said as he straightened up. Sadie wanted to scream but it caught in her throat, and she continued to wordlessly follow her father even though her whole body was shaking now with an icy fear that penetrated all the way to her bones.

The prints were getting bloodier and bloodier, until they reached the end of the trail and suddenly the prints just vanished into thin air.

Then the screaming started.

A young girl's voice, screaming in pain and terror, echoed through the trees and Sadie's throat unfroze as she recognized who that voice belonged to and screamed in return.

It was Jessica...

... "Sadie! Sadie. Wake up."

Sadie sat bolt upright in bed, still screaming. Her eyes wide and frantic, she struggled for a moment with the hands that were shaking her, seeing bear's paws, until her vision cleared, and she saw that it was Caz, gazing down at her in concern.

"Oh my God. I'm all right, I'm all right," she muttered, pulling her knees up to her chest and rubbing her eyes as she adjusted to reality.

"That was one hell of a nightmare," Caz said matter-of-factly. Sadie nodded weakly.

"Yeah, I get them sometimes."

"I know," Caz said. Sadie realized that Caz must have heard her crying out in the night before. Ever since her return to Alaska, her nightmares about Jessica were getting more and more frequent.

"I'm sorry," she said, feeling embarrassed being caught in such a vulnerable state. "I didn't mean to wake you."

"You didn't," Caz reassured her. "It's six a.m., I was already getting up. Your phone was ringing, you left it in the kitchen. It was the sheriff; there's been another bear attack."

Sadie shuddered at Caz's words, remembering the scene from her dream, but then as she processed what her friend was saying she peered at her in confusion.

"Why was he calling me?" Cooper had made it abundantly clear what he had thought about her theory that the attack was somehow staged.

"I don't know, hon. Why don't you ask him? I'll go and make us some coffee. You look like you need some."

Sadie nodded gratefully as Caz left the room, staring at her cell phone for a few moments before she dialed the sheriff's number. She couldn't fathom why he would want to tell her about the second bear attack. Maybe to show her that her theory was wrong, and there really was a killer bear on the rampage? But it wasn't like Cooper to gloat, and certainly not before six in the morning.

"Price. Thanks for calling me back." Cooper sounded tired when he answered her call and Sadie wondered how long he had been at the scene.

"No worries. What's up?" She swung her legs over the edge of the bed and paced across the room toward the small window. She could see the mountains in the distance, and she bit at her lip as vivid scenes from her dream came to mind once more.

"There's been another bear attack," he said. He sounded uncertain, almost as though he was regretting calling her, or second-guessing his own reasons as to why.

"Okay," Sadie said slowly as the sheriff paused, and she heard him sigh.

"You know I don't believe a word of your crazy theory about Marie DuVale's death being more than a wild animal attack, right?" he said, and Sadie instantly understood what it was that he wanted of her.

"You've found reason to believe this attack is staged too, haven't you?" she asked bluntly.

"Maybe," Cooper said after a long pause. "It's the same type of set-up…food was left lying around. There are chicken bones outside, almost as though someone had left food on the path to the cabin."

"A trail," Sadie said flatly, although her mind was working overtime. It couldn't be a coincidence, and anyone living up in that neck of the words should know all of the safety procedures. Clearing up food scraps was the first thing anyone staying or living in bear country was told to do to keep safe.

"It looks that way," Cooper said cautiously. "We've got Bonsor on his way here, and Pete of course, but I don't expect that they will find anything other than yet another wild animal attack. In fact, I'm probably being insane even considering your crackpot idea. You've put the image of a trail in my head. I'm seeing things that aren't there."

"Yet you want me to come and take a look at the thing you're seeing that's not there, so that I can tell you it is there, and then you can tell me I'm crazy," Sadie said, trying not to smile. She was already tugging on her pants.

"Something like that," Cooper said, although he sounded more puzzled than amused. "The thing is, Price, I can't just go around throwing wild accusations out there, especially if McAllister is involved. But I've worked with you on two major cases now and I've seen how shit-hot your instincts are. God help me, but I can't completely rule this out. Come and take a look, will you? But don't say too much to the others. Not unless something concrete turns up...even though it won't, of course."

Sadie could almost feel sorry for the sheriff. He was clearly battling his own internal conflict by asking her to come and cast an eye over this. She was flattered by his comment about her instincts though, enough that her voice softened as she replied.

"I'll be there as soon as I can. And I'll be discreet, although I don't know what reason you're going to give for calling me in."

"I'm the sheriff. I don't need a reason," he said. Sadie smiled again as she ended the call.

Her smile soon disappeared as she dressed, grabbed her gun, and headed out to her truck. Sheriff Cooper might still be decidedly wary of the idea, but as far as Sadie was concerned, this was now an active murder investigation.

And it was a human, not a bear, that she would now be hunting.

*

Rick was already at the cabin by the time Sadie arrived. As she pulled up and saw his Jeep, she felt the low burn of desire in her gut that didn't abate when she swiftly tried to quash it.

She seriously needed to get a grip if she was going to end up working on these attacks. Rick Bonsor was a distraction that she had no time for right now, even if part of her thought that he would be a very welcome distraction indeed.

The second cabin belonged to a woman called Jane Winters, who after the death of her husband had moved out here to the cabin that they both owned and become something of a recluse. She used to be a teacher in Anchorage, and occasionally still traveled into town to help out at the junior high, or to do some private tutoring.

As she entered the now deceased teacher's cabin Sadie held her breath, preparing herself for both the sight and the smell that she knew was about to hit her. Sure enough, the scene was as gory as the first.

"Price," Cooper said, looking relieved. Rick only nodded in greeting, but she saw his eyes light up in appreciation. Sadie looked away quickly, feeling her cheeks go warm and hoping the sheriff wouldn't notice her immediate reaction to the handsome zoologist. Or his to her.

Not that it was any of Cooper's business, she reminded herself.

"Who called this in, was it Carson again?" she asked. It was Rick who answered her.

"I did," he said. "I was out here tracking bear activity. Early morning is a good time for it. I saw the door had been busted off and checked it out...then I called the sheriff and went to try and track the bear. I had no luck, so I came back here."

"He—or she—didn't leave a trail?" Sadie asked, and immediately thought of large pawprints filled with blood.

"Yes...but then it hit the river," Rick said. Cooper looked at him.

"We can't wait any longer, Bonsor," he grumbled. "I know you have a job to do, but so do I, and two attacks in less than twenty-four hours is unheard of. We have to set up a hunt and take the beast down before it kills anyone else. It clearly has a taste for human flesh that goes way beyond hunger."

Rick nodded reluctantly, although he looked upset. For a moment, Sadie almost wondered if the bear expert had lost the trail on purpose. She couldn't see him ever killing one of the creatures.

"What happened here, Rick?" she asked as she looked around the gore-strewn cabin, nodding at Pete who was methodically cataloging limbs. "Could you talk me through a bear attack? Or, more specifically, *this* bear attack?"

Rick looked surprised, but if the zoologist was wondering why an FBI behavioral expert was asking questions at the scene of an animal attack, he was polite enough not to voice it.

"Sure. If you look back out onto the path, you can see a few scraps of bone. There are a few more over there by the trees. I'm guessing from that Winters was careless, was eating something on her way home perhaps, and chucked the bones. If there's a bear sniffing around, particularly one who has already had a successful hunt around here, it would have been like a red rag to a bull."

Sadie glanced at Cooper, who she knew would be thinking the exact same thing as her. Winters was native to Alaska and had lived in this cabin for a few years. Would she really have been so careless as to toss bones around outside her cabin? Would Marie DuVale have been?

Sadie didn't think her theory was at all unlikely anymore. Or at least, it was less unlikely than this happening twice in less than twenty-four hours. Once could be a tragic accident, but twice was the beginning of a pattern.

"So, the bear made its way into the cabin and then just attacked? Is that typical...I mean, wouldn't it need to be provoked?" Sadie asked,

41

wishing she could remember everything she had been told about bears as a kid.

"Bears will usually only attack under provocation," Rick agreed. "But the problem is that they consider most human reactions to them to be a provocation. If Winters or DuVale had screamed, or reached for a weapon, or tried to run…that would be enough for a grizzly to attack. And remember, it came in looking for food. Humans are food, and definitely tastier than anything that could be found in the victim's cupboard."

Sadie absorbed the information, trying not to think about DuVale's and Winters's terrifying last moments as the bear sunk in its teeth and ripped them apart. It would have been quick at least, she consoled herself. She had seen much worse, and bears, she supposed, were just being bears. There was no deliberate evil in their actions.

If someone had led the bear straight to its prey, however, then that was inescapably evil. Not to mention cowardly. Sadie was used to killers who took a perverse pleasure in killing their victims. This wasn't personal; this was about something specific that the victims were simply on the periphery of.

Like a coveted land development that was set to make billions in profit. Winters's cabin wasn't very far from DuVale's. That would put her in the highlighted zone too. And if this cabin meant something to Jane Winters, reminding her of her deceased husband, then what were the chances that she would want to sell?

"Will the bear continue to return to the area?" Cooper spoke up, interrupting Sadie's thoughts. "Now that it has successfully killed here twice? So much for bear attacks on humans supposedly being rare."

"They are rare," Rick corrected him. "Bears aren't usually a threat, Sheriff. These two women were careless. But to answer your question, yes, it will most likely return now. This could become its prime hunting ground, in fact. You need to evacuate the area."

Sadie winced at the tone in Rick's words, as though he thoroughly expected Sheriff Cooper to do as he said. Cooper was an amiable enough guy most days, but he didn't take kindly to anyone stepping on his turf, as Sadie knew from experience, and there was clearly no love lost between him and the animal expert.

"Do I now?" Cooper murmured; his voice low enough that it was almost a growl. "I think I'm in charge of those decisions, Bonsor. Before I have to tell people to evacuate their homes in the middle of winter, we can take down this bear."

"I understand," Rick said, although he sounded impatient. "But I have more work to do before I can be sure of the bear we're looking for."

"You've had time, Bonsor," Cooper said angrily, "and all we have is another dead woman on our hands. I don't have any love for killing innocent animals either as I said before, but I won't prioritize the life of a bear over that of a human. If we have to kill more animals than necessary to save human lives, then so be it."

The expression on Rick's face was akin to if Cooper had just spouted blasphemy in front of a preacher. Sadie wandered outside to examine the ground around the cabin, leaving the two of them to argue it out amongst themselves. It wasn't the bear hunt that was her concern.

It was discovering who had led the bear here, and why. She walked around the periphery of the cabin, carefully combing the ground. If Rick or Pete had asked what she was doing, she could say that she was examining the bear tracks, or the scraps of food that had enticed the creature, but it was the tracks of a car rather than that of an animal that Sadie was looking for.

Sure enough, she found them amongst the trees, just a few meters from Jane Winters's cabin. Fresh tracks in the snow, as though someone had been here just a few hours before. Around the time of the bear attack, perhaps.

She was no tire track expert, but judging by the size and tread, they belonged to one of the newer Jeeps rather than the locally favored snow trucks. As far as she was concerned, this was no coincidence.

She needed to talk to George McAllister, and this time she wasn't taking no for an answer.

CHAPTER NINE

As they drove toward the business park and the Clarity Land Development site in Cooper's snowcat, the sheriff was quiet, but he seemed tense. Sadie looked over at him, noticing the tight grip of his hands on the steering wheel.

"You're worried about interviewing McAllister, aren't you?" she guessed.

"Some," the sheriff admitted. "When I said he was a major player around here, I wasn't exaggerating. He could cause me a fair amount of trouble if he decides to."

"I can do this by myself, Cooper," Sadie offered. "Then you can just blame me."

The sheriff shook his head. "No," he said firmly. "I invited you to the second attack because I wanted your opinion. And if there is even the tiniest chance that you're onto something here, then we can't afford to ignore it."

"But you don't think there is, not really," Sadie guessed. Cooper took his eyes off the road ahead for a second to flash her a wry smile.

"No, I don't," he conceded. "In fact, I'm battling with myself as to whether I've gone as crazy as you to even consider it. But you're right, it's odd. Two attacks, what looks like a trail at both cabins, and they're both in a planned development zone and McAllister is at the scene? We need to talk to him at least."

"That's all we're doing," Sadie reminded him. "We're not going in there with guns drawn, threatening to haul his ass down to the station."

Cooper grinned at that. "But you would if you could, Price."

"Maybe." Sadie grinned back.

They pulled into the business park. It was still early, and people were just beginning to arrive for the workday. Sadie wondered if McAllister would even be in the office yet, but as they approached the Clarity building, she saw his distinctive black Jeep parked in his CEO reserved spot.

"He's here."

"Let's get this over with," Cooper sighed as he jumped out of the vehicle.

As they entered the reception area the same woman Sadie had spoken to the day before looked over and opened her mouth in surprise as she spotted them. She immediately picked up the phone in front of her. To warn McAllister?

Sadie quickened her pace in order to reach the reception, but Cooper laid a hand on her arm.

"Is that the survey that you were telling me about?" He motioned discreetly toward the map that Sadie had seen the day before. She nodded and the sheriff walked over to it. Reckoning that the receptionist would have spoken to McAllister by now, she followed the sheriff, who stood in front of the land survey, peering closely at the highlighted area.

"What are you thinking?" she asked.

"I'm just wondering how many cabins fall into this area," he murmured. "How many people would need to be persuaded to sell up by Clarity. It's a bit much to think that they could all be mysteriously devoured by a bear."

"They wouldn't need to be," Sadie countered. "What better way to convince people to want to move? No one wants to be in the path of a rampaging grizzly."

"But couldn't that backfire?" Cooper said. "If the area gets that sort of reputation, would tourists really want to visit a resort there?"

Sadie was pondering that when she saw a man stride past on the other side of the room, glancing over at them as he all but ran out of the glass doors.

"Cooper," she whispered urgently, already moving to follow the man. "That's McAllister. He's leaving."

The sheriff was right behind her, hurrying out into the parking lot where McAllister was about to get into his Jeep.

"Mr. McAllister?" Cooper called. "We would just like to ask you a few questions." His voice carried clearly over the parking lot, but McAllister made no signs of having heard them and got into his vehicle. Cooper called him again, but the CEO only slammed his door shut and started the engine.

"Shit," Cooper exclaimed. "He's actually going to make a run for it." Sadie was already sprinting toward the snowcat. If McAllister was running, then there had to be a good reason why.

They followed him out of the business park, and he continued to show no sign of having even noticed them, in spite of Sadie waving in his rearview mirror. Cooper's vehicle was clearly marked as belonging to the local sheriff, so there was no doubt that McAllister was purposely ignoring them.

As soon as they were out on the open road, McAllister sped up dramatically. Hesitating for only a second, Cooper sped up after him and turned the sirens on.

"Son of a bitch," he said through gritted teeth. "Why doesn't he just stop?"

"Because he's guilty of something," Sadie said. "Or so arrogant that he thinks the rules don't apply to him."

"He needs to slow down," Cooper said, yanking the wheel hard as the snowcat veered to the side as it hit a snowbank. "The roads around here are in no state for a chase."

"He seems to be heading toward the coast," Sadie said with a frown. "What the hell is he playing at?"

"An escape on his luxury yacht seems a bit dramatic," Cooper said drily.

Not if you're responsible for the deaths of two women, Sadie thought. There could be surely no other explanation for McAllister's behavior. He was either somehow responsible for those bear attacks, or he knew something.

If they could just get him to pull over, they might be able to find out what that was.

The snowcat's tires made a screech that could be heard above the sirens as it skidded on a patch of black ice, and Sadie gripped the side of the seat. The last time she and Sheriff Cooper had been in hazardous conditions like this, the vehicle had overturned, and Cooper had been lucky to escape with his life. She wasn't eager for a repeat situation. Cooper, however, was now as suspicious of McAllister as she was and determined to catch the land developer.

He hit the gas.

As they gained on McAllister the man seemed to panic and suddenly veered his Jeep to the side. For a moment, Sadie thought he had lost control of his vehicle, but then realized that he was deliberately going over the embankment in a bid to lose them. She shook her head at the man's stupidity. His Jeep might be new and flashy, but the sheriff's snowcat was expertly built for these conditions.

Even so, Sadie issued a warning as the sheriff turned the wheel to follow McAllister.

"There's a steep drop here if you go too far down, Cooper."

"I know that," Cooper responded. "I'm just wondering if he does. Or we could well be held responsible for running him off the road. If it turns out he's done nothing wrong."

"Only guilty men run like this," Sadie argued. Then she inhaled sharply as she jolted forward in her seat as Cooper veered sharply around a tree. This was getting dangerous, and McAllister seemed to have no idea where he was actually heading but was just blindly trying to lose them. He was at the top of an icy verge now and Sadie held her breath. His Jeep was too close to the edge.

"He's going to go over," Cooper said, just as the Jeep skidded on a patch of ice. Sadie watched in horror as if in slow motion the Jeep spun around and went backwards down the embankment, completely out of control.

Cursing, Cooper stopped the snowcat and jumped out to follow the Jeep. Sadie followed, half running and half falling down the steep hill. A few meters below them the Jeep had mercifully run into a large snowbank and come to a standstill without too much damage being done—to the vehicle at least. There was no sign of movement from inside. Sadie held her breath, praying that McAllister wasn't dead.

Sheriff Cooper wouldn't thank her if the outcome of this was him being held responsible for the death of one of Anchorage's political bigshots, even if it turned out that the man was indeed guilty of staging the women's deaths.

She exhaled with relief as they approached the Jeep and heard a moan from inside.

"McAllister?" Cooper called, his hand on his gun as he approached the vehicle. "Are you hurt?"

There was a muffled response from inside. As Sadie clambered through the snow to reach the passenger side window, she saw that the airbag had inflated on the driver's side, saving McAllister from the impact of the sudden stop.

Cooper helped him out of the Jeep, and whatever instinct had propelled the man to flee had been crushed by the shock of the crash. He stood meekly looking down at his ridiculously expensive shoes, which were worse than useless in this snow.

"Why did you run?" Sadie asked. "We just wanted to ask you a few questions."

"I panicked," McAllister said, not looking at her. His demeanor was that of a naughty kid who had been caught doing something he shouldn't, Sadie thought, rather than that of someone who was capable of arranging for women to be mauled by a hungry bear. Still, she knew from experience that appearances could be deceiving.

"Well, you don't seem to be hurt," Cooper said shortly. "So, unless you think you need medical attention, maybe you can come to the station and explain to me just why you panicked?"

McAllister nodded glumly and followed Sadie meekly to the snowcat. As Cooper drove off toward the station, Sadie looked back at the man in the rearview mirror. *He isn't the right guy,* she thought, even though she was still certain that trails had been laid for the bear. But if not, then why was he at the scene? And what would he have to panic about? It didn't make any sense.

Because if McAllister wasn't the killer, that meant he was still out there.

CHAPTER TEN

Sadie sat opposite McAllister in the interrogation room, watching him sip on a mug of coffee. He was wrapped in a blanket they had found in reception, left by the state trooper who had been on the night shift. Now that he was warm, and the shock of the crash was wearing off, McAllister was displaying some of the arrogance that Sadie would have expected from a CEO and close friend of the mayor.

"Before we ask our questions, I have to advise you that you might want to call your lawyer," the sheriff said, sounding more formal than Sadie had come to expect from him. She knew he was still nervous about being seen to accuse McAllister of murder with so little evidence to go on. The man potentially had enough clout to cost Cooper his job.

And maybe hers, too, Sadie realized. She wondered how politically connected her ASAC, Paul Golightly, was.

McAllister raised an eyebrow, looking coolly at the sheriff. "Do I need one? I thought this was just a few questions? Helping with inquiries?"

"It is. I have to advise you as a formality," Cooper said carefully. McAllister shrugged nonchalantly.

"There's no need," he said. "I hope this isn't going to take very long."

You weren't so confident when you were running away in your Jeep, Sadie thought, narrowing her eyes as she looked at him, trying to get a feel for what he could be hiding. People didn't speed away from the cops for no reason.

"We hope not," Cooper said politely. "Do you know why we wanted to talk to you?"

"I'm assuming," McAllister said, and Sadie saw a flash of fear in his eyes, "that it has something to do with the women who were attacked in their cabins? Because your agent here turned up at my offices yesterday right after the first one was killed, demanding that she speak to me without making an appointment. I don't know why you think it has anything to do with me."

"I'm not the sheriff's agent," Sadie cut in calmly. "I'm an FBI behavioral specialist, assisting on this case. And if you are so clueless as to why we want to talk to you, why did you run? Or rather, drive so fast that you damn near killed yourself? I don't need to be an expert to know that makes a man look guilty."

Cooper shot her a sideways look and Sadie knew he was warning her to go easy on the man, but Sadie was getting annoyed by his casual arrogance. She was about to speak again when McAllister interrupted her.

"You're with the Anchorage field office then? You must work under Golightly? He's a good man, I know him very well."

Sadie felt anger at the obvious attempt to psych her out. She smiled tightly.

"I'll tell him you said hello. Now, can you answer my question? Why drive away from us like that if you have nothing to do with the attacks? And before you answer you might want to know that I saw you at Marie DuVale's cabin yesterday, and I know you were at Jane Winters's cabin before the attack this morning."

McAllister looked genuinely surprised. "I wasn't there, not this morning," he protested. "I was in bed, my wife can vouch for that, she's an early riser."

"We saw the tracks," Sadie argued. McAllister smirked, and Sadie had to fight the urge to wipe it off his face. She had no time for this.

"That's your evidence? I'm not the only one who drives a Jeep like that."

"What about yesterday?" she fired back. "I saw you there, watching the cabin, and followed you back to your offices. So, what would be your explanation for that?"

McAllister looked down and then sighed heavily. "I didn't know you were FBI yesterday," he said. "I saw you come out of the cabin and see me there, but I thought you were just a wildlife ranger or something. Until my receptionist told me."

"Unlucky for you," she retorted. "So, why were you there?"

McAllister was silent for a long moment before he answered, and now he sounded slightly defeated, his cockiness ebbing away.

"Look, I had nothing to do with the women being attacked," he said, his eyes pleading with them to believe him. "I don't know the first thing about bears. But then I found out you were FBI, and then this morning I heard about the second attack on the radio on the way to work and then suddenly you're there with the sheriff. I just panicked, like I said."

"Why?" Cooper spoke up, leaning forward. "What did you have to panic about?"

McAllister looked down at his hands, and Sadie thought he looked ashamed.

"Marie was refusing to sell," he said. "She just wouldn't budge on it, no matter what great offers we came up with, so in the end I had been trying to persuade her myself. The last time I spoke to her was only a few days ago and it got quite heated. I tried to explain to her that I know people. In the publishing industry."

"So," Cooper said coldly, "you threatened to damage her career if she didn't do what you wanted?"

"Persuasion, Sheriff," McAllister said. "If you can't persuade people to buy what you're selling with incentives, then you go for the pain points. I'm a businessman," he said, as though that excused him.

"Okay," Sadie said, "so that's why you ran?"

McAllister looked down at his feet again. "She threatened to have me arrested for harassment," he admitted. "I'm sure you can see how that would damage my reputation. I went back yesterday to have one last try at persuading her, but when I turned up you were already there, Sheriff. I hung around a bit to see what was going on. I didn't realize it was an animal attack at first. It's all very shocking."

There was silence in the interrogation room as they digested his confession. Cooper looked at her, and she knew he was silently wondering if she believed the land developer's story.

"What about Jane Winters?" Sadie pressed.

"I told you, I wasn't there earlier," McAllister insisted, sounding annoyed that she was still questioning him. "I had no need to be. Winters had already agreed to sell up. We sent her the contract a few days ago. You can check that out with my office."

"Oh, we will," Sadie assured him. She avoided looking at Cooper, knowing that her theory was falling apart. If McAllister's alibi checked out and so did Winters's contract, then they really had no case against him.

But that didn't mean that she was wrong about the attacks looking staged, she thought stubbornly.

"You really think that they weren't just attacks?" McAllister asked, echoing her thoughts. He sounded eager for the information, and Sadie wondered which scenario would be most likely to negatively affect Clarity's plans for a five-star resort. Bear attacks were likely to simply scare people away, but a human killer? Sadie knew that perversely, people were often drawn to such things, and the gorier and more horrific the better.

Some days, Sadie thought that the more she understood about humanity's dark side, the less she wanted to be around people.

Could that be a motive? She eyed McAllister, wondering if he was deranged enough to set up the whole thing just to draw in tourists with an eye for the macabre. It was even more far-fetched than her first theory, she acknowledged to herself, but even so, she wasn't going to write McAllister off as a suspect just yet, whatever Sheriff Cooper said.

"We are looking into all possibilities," the sheriff said evenly. "Well, if that's all, then thank you for helping us with our inquiries. I'll get someone to take you back to your Jeep and help dig it out." Cooper was all cold politeness toward the man now.

"Hang on," McAllister said. "You should know…if you're looking for a suspect, you should look closer to home. That hunter, or whatever he is, Bobby Carson, I always saw him hanging around the cabins. Around the women. Jane told me she found him creepy. I'm not saying he had anything to do with it, but, well, he knows about wildlife."

"Thank you," Cooper said, standing up. "We'll make a note of that."

He showed the CEO out while Sadie stayed sat in the room, thinking. She had felt immediately suspicious of Carson, but what could his motive possibly be? Not that the worst killers had a motive that anyone else would necessarily understand, but serial killers generally liked to be hands on, not use bears.

Unless, she thought, he had killed them and then lured the bears in to get rid of the evidence. She made a mental note to ask Rick if bears would eat a fresh corpse and tear it apart.

Even in the midst of an interrogation the thought of Rick Bonsor made her feel warm.

Cooper came back into the room, looking ill at ease.

"You're thinking that you shouldn't have listened to me, aren't you?" Sadie sighed. To her surprise, Cooper shook his head.

"No, I'm not. In fact, I'm starting to get creeped out by this too. But I'm not worried about McAllister. He won't want it to come out that he was harassing Marie DuVale and hanging around near the time of the attack. Gossip flies fast around here."

Sadie nodded, feeling relieved. She stood up, suddenly unsure what to do with herself. Going back to the saloon didn't appeal, but neither did checking in at the field office early. That only left going to the hospital and sitting next to her still comatose father, and she just wasn't sure that she could face it.

"You have the bear hunt today?" she asked.

"Yes, I'm going to assemble it now. Bonsor is insisting on coming—no doubt to protect as many of his precious bears as he can."

"You need him to identify which one he thinks is the manhunter," Sadie pointed out. She knew that Cooper wouldn't want Rick around even if he was the best bear hunter in the state. It was strange that they had instantly hated each other, she mused, because in some ways they struck her as very alike.

Men.

"Yeah," Cooper said, sounding as though he would rather take his chances than rely on the zoologist's expertise. "Listen, Price," he added, "do you want to continue with the inquiries while we are all out on the hunt? In light of what McAllister told us?"

Sadie was taken aback. "You still think they were staged?" She was pleased that the sheriff was still taking her seriously. He shrugged.

"Maybe not, but like I said, it's creeping me out. Can't hurt to be cautious. I was thinking you could check Winters's cabin over and ask around about Carson supposedly sleazing around the women. It's probably unrelated but...who knows? And it will keep you busy. I know you will just be driving yourself crazy worrying about your father, even if you don't want to admit it." He looked away almost shyly, expecting Sadie to snap, but despite herself she felt touched at his concern.

And he was right. She needed something to do. She followed him back outside and into the snowcat. She had left her truck by Winters's cabin when they had followed after McAllister. Cooper drove in silence, his eyes on the road. Sadie wondered how he felt about the upcoming bear hunt and shuddered as images of her dream came to mind.

It had seemed so real...

What if she was just overtired? If she was leading Cooper on a wild goose chase looking for a killer that didn't exist? Wasting their time on something that was completely straightforward. Sadie knew that she had just had a rough few months, and now with her father's sudden collapse, she could be forgiven for not thinking straight.

That would be the logical explanation.

But illogical or not, Sadie felt certain that there was more to this case than met the eye, and it was a pressing feeling, not just a vague hunch.

And if she was right, that meant there was a killer on the loose.

Which meant that no matter the outcome of this bear hunt, there would be more deaths, and another body.

CHAPTER ELEVEN

As Sadie and the sheriff arrived back at Jane Winters's cabin, Pete was just leaving with the woman's body—or what was left of it—in a body bag, ready to go to the morgue. He passed the keys to Cooper, who passed them to Sadie.

"Have a look around; I'll wait outside for the hunt to arrive. Don't lose those keys; we haven't located any next of kin yet and there doesn't seem to be a spare set."

Sadie nodded at him and was about to enter the cabin when she spotted Bobby Carson through the window. Through the open inner doors, she could see that he was in the bedroom with his back to her. He was standing over a dresser, reaching into his backpack, and for a moment she assumed that he was stealing something.

Then she watched him open a drawer and place a scrap of cloth inside and realized that he wasn't stealing anything at all.

He was putting something back.

Stepping away from the window so that she didn't alert Carson to her presence, she walked over to Pete and lowered her voice as she spoke. The ME was just about to get into his truck, but he looked up with a tired smile as Sadie approached.

"I hope you get the beast today," he said. "I don't want to scrape up any more brains, to be quite honest."

Sadie winced at the mental image.

"What is Carson doing in there?" she asked.

"Bobby? Oh, he was just hanging around, asking a few questions in preparation for the hunt. He wanted to know if I could tell the size of the bear's claws, that sort of thing. I think he fancies himself as some sort of expert."

"Thanks, Pete," Sadie said, mulling over his words. She walked into the cabin to see Carson walking out of the bedroom. He was visibly startled as he saw Sadie.

"Agent? Aren't you going on the hunt?"

"I'm just checking everything is in order before we lock the place up," Sadie replied. She looked pointedly at Carson's backpack, and he shifted from one foot to the other under her gaze, unable to meet her eyes. "I'm not sure why you are here, though?"

"I was just giving Pete a hand…as you and the sheriff drove off so quickly," he retorted. Sadie raised an eyebrow.

"And that involved you going into Ms. Winters's bedroom, did it?"

Pete swallowed, his eyes darting around the cabin. "I was just wondering if the bear went in there too."

And had a rifle through her panties? Sadie thought but decided not to say. She wanted to have a look around before she told Carson that she had caught him in the act of returning what had looked highly likely to be an item of underwear.

As Carson walked past her to go outside, Sadie called him back. "I was just talking to Pete," she said conversationally. "He said that you had a lot of questions about the bear. I was just wondering why that was?"

Carson looked surprised. "I was trying to help," he said innocently. "You can't be a trapper your whole life and not know a thing or two about bears. I bet I know more than that hotshot university guy anyway," he said dismissively. Sadie wondered if there was any man who didn't become immediately competitive around Rick Bonsor.

"Right. Well, you shouldn't really be in here. If you want to go outside, you can wait with the sheriff. There's a guy coming from Game and Wildlife to lead the hunt."

Carson hesitated for a moment, looking as though he had more to say, but then he changed his mind and left hurriedly. Sadie watched him go, shut the cabin door behind him, and headed straight into Jane Winters's bedroom.

It was clean and tidy, a jarring juxtaposition to the chaos that the bear had left in the next room. A framed photograph of Winter and her late husband stood on the dresser that she had seen Carson rifling through. She opened the top drawer, grimacing when she saw it was, as she had suspected, full of underwear. Smart, simple cotton, nothing fancy, arranged in neat rows, except for one crumpled pair flung hurriedly on the top.

They must be the pair that Carson was replacing, she thought. Reaching into her own backpack for gloves and a baggie, she carefully took the panties as evidence.

Evidence of what exactly, other than Carson being a low-grade pervert, she wasn't sure.

There was a computer desk on the other side of the room underneath the window, and Sadie looked through its unlocked drawer next. Face up on top of a pile of papers was a contract showing a letterhead she recognized.

Clarity Land Development. A quick flick through seemed to conform McAllister's story, but Sadie took that as evidence too, if only to completely rule him out as a suspect.

Not that there were any official suspects. She knew that the deaths would be ruled as straightforward, if gruesome, bear attacks, and unless she found more concrete evidence than some tire tracks and a crumpled pair of panties, it was going to stay that way.

At the bottom of the pile of paper was a diary. Sadie hesitated before picking it up. There was something so intimate about a diary or journal, and without an official investigation underway Sadie felt reluctant to invade the dead woman's privacy in such a way. Still, it might shine more light on Winters's involvement with both McAllister and Carson.

She was about to take the diary out when she heard the roar of engines outside and the chatter of male voices along with the barking of sled dogs. The sheriff called to her from the main room, his boots thudding across the wooden floor.

"Are you coming along, Price?" he asked, then in a lower voice, "Did you find anything?"

She fished the contract and panties out of her bag. "It seems McAllister was telling the truth about the contract with Jane Winters, at least. And he wasn't wrong about Carson hanging around...I'm guessing from this that he was attempting to return these in case anyone noticed they were missing. Although why he thinks we would be inventorying her underwear I don't know."

Cooper shook his head in disgust. "The son of a bitch," he swore. "So you think he had an obsession with Winters?"

"Perhaps not just her," Sadie said thoughtfully. "McAllister seemed to think he was hanging around the women in general. I wonder if he was taking items from Marie DuVale as well."

They met each other's eyes, and Sadie could see the sheriff was thinking hard, turning it all over in his head. At some point, she realized, they had gone from speculating that there was something odd about this case to treating it as a murder investigation.

"I could go and check her cabin out too," Sadie suggested. "I'll start off joining the hunt and then slip away. Doesn't Carson have a trapper's cabin around here? It might be open—I could check that out too, see if any of the women's items are there. That will give us enough reason to bring him in for questioning if I find anything."

Cooper looked unsure. "Carson's place is up by the headwaters...it could be dangerous."

"I'm armed. I'll be careful," she said, but Cooper shook his head.

"I don't want you taking unnecessary risks for this," he insisted. Sadie nodded as though she was agreeing, but Cooper looked unconvinced. He knew how stubborn she was…and also that he had no real authority to tell her what not to do. As an FBI agent, she didn't fall under Cooper's command. It was a fact that had caused not a small amount of tension on the previous two cases that they had worked together.

She followed him outside, where the hunt was raring to go. Ten local men, including Carson, and a heavyset man in a deep brown Game and Wildlife uniform, holding the leashes of three large, growling dogs. The sight made her shudder, and she couldn't help feeling a pang of compassion for the animal that was about to be hunted down, no matter how ferocious it was.

The eager look on the faces of the men almost turned Sadie's stomach. She had been a part of teams determinedly hunting down some of the most depraved killers in society and had never seen this naked bloodlust that she saw on the faces of the hunters.

Were they really any better than the bears?

The Game and Wildlife guy walked over to them and pumped Cooper's hand. He was tall and broad with a bald head, a black bushy beard, and penetrating green eyes. Sadie watched him and the sheriff assessing each other and fought the urge to simultaneously sigh and roll her eyes. There was way too much testosterone around here.

"Billy Garcia," the man introduced himself. He turned to Sadie, his eyes flicking up and down her body unashamedly. "You must be Deputy Cooper?"

Before Sadie could answer with a cutting reply of her own, the sheriff replied for her. "My sister is busy on another case. This is Special Agent Sadie Price."

Garcia looked taken aback…and, Sadie thought, slightly angry. "Why do we need a Fed here?" he asked bluntly.

"I'm here as a concerned local," Sadie said evenly. Garcia looked unimpressed.

"You've been on hunts before?"

"Yes," she said shortly, deciding that now wasn't the time to mention that she had been on one bear hunt, and as a kid.

"Okay," Garcia said, although he looked less than pleased by her presence. "As long as you understand I'm in charge here. I'll be heading up the hunt with Carson, who I understand knows the area best. The sheriff will take the rear. You can stick with him, Miss Price."

"It's *Agent* Price," Sadie said, ice in her voice, but Garcia had already walked away and was barking orders to the rest of the men.

There was no sign of Rick, and although she felt disappointed Sadie wondered if it was a good thing. Garcia, Cooper, Carson, and Rick all vying with each other to be in charge of the situation was only going to cause fireworks.

"Where's Rick?" she asked casually, looking innocently at Cooper when his eyes narrowed with suspicion.

"He's gone off alone, making impressions of pawprints to match to the crime scene," he said. "Still trying to make sure we get the right bear."

"Makes sense." Sadie shrugged. "We don't want to kill any more animals than necessary."

"Tell that to this lot," Cooper murmured as a cheer went up from the assembled men as Garcia announced they were ready to begin.

Garcia and Carson took the lead as he had said, with the others fanning out behind. Using the information Carson and the sheriff had given him, Garcia announced that they would head straight for the headwaters at the gorge.

"Don't wander off, Price," Cooper warned.

"I thought we agreed I would look over DuVale's cabin?" she said innocently. "I may as well check out Carson's place if I get the chance. I might not, but if I do…"

Cooper just gave an exasperated sigh as they headed off and Sadie followed, smiling to herself.

She was glad to have something to do, and to have another lead to chase. Carson's behavior was undoubtedly out of the ordinary, and if he had developed an obsession with the women, it might just be possible that had darkened into something more dangerous. Perhaps they had rejected him, or threatened to report him? Sexual obsession was often a powerful motive for murder.

Sadie's mind was on her own hunt as she followed Garcia's lead, and when the dogs picked up a scent that meant they were veering away from the headwaters Sadie hung back before slipping off through the trails to make her own way to the headwaters…and Carson's cabin.

She was so lost in her own thoughts that she didn't hear the footsteps behind her.

CHAPTER TWELVE

Sadie was moving up the gorge toward Carson's ramshackle trapper's cabin when she became aware of the bear. It was to the left and slightly behind her, and she sensed its eyes on her before she saw it.

She stood still, trying to calm her breathing and reminding herself that most bears didn't come near humans. That as long as it didn't perceive her as a threat then she would be fine. But it was far from easy trying to convince herself of that when she had just witnessed two women who had been torn apart.

What if this was that same bear?

It didn't look particularly savage; its stride was long and loping and it sniffed the air as it moved, seemingly not too concerned by Sadie's presence. She didn't get the impression that it was about to charge her, but then what would she know? She was no bear expert.

It certainly could be the killer. It was huge, a deep chocolate brown in color, its coat sleek and the muscles rippling powerfully beneath its skin. Sadie tried to remember everything she knew about encountering bears in the wild.

Don't run. That was the most important thing. Running would only encourage it to chase, and there was no outrunning a grizzly bear.

Don't make eye contact. Bears, like dogs, would perceive direct eye contact as a threat. Sadie looked into the distance, trying to relax and keep her breathing even. She reminded herself that if it came to it, she was armed. She wasn't helpless, as Marie DuVale and Jane Winters had been. There was no need to panic.

Even though it could take a good few bullets to stop a grizzly, and it could do plenty of damage within that time.

Walk away slowly. Sadie continued to walk toward the cabin, at an angle to the bear so that she wasn't quite turning her back to it but could just make out its shape out of the corner of her eye. The bear would lose any interest in her, she told herself firmly, and carry on about its way.

But that wasn't what happened. As Sadie moved toward the cabin the bear picked up its stride and was now heading directly toward her. Unable to help herself, Sadie moved quicker, her eyes resolutely on the cabin in front of her as though that could offer her any kind of shelter against an aggressive grizzly. Her hand was on her holster, ready to draw.

Then she heard the bear break into a run.

Sadie spun around on the path, her gun raised, about to fire into the bear's chest, but the grizzly was so close that she turned around and nearly crashed straight into it. The bear reached for her, swiping at her with its great paw. It felt as though she had been run over by a truck as she flew off the path and landed on the icy rock of the gorge, her gun flying from her hand and falling meters away near the headwaters of the river.

The thought flashed through her mind, as sharp as a razor blade: *I'm going to die.*

But the bear wasn't upon her. It had circled away and was now coming back toward her, its gait slow and menacing.

It was going to attack.

Play dead. That was the advice in event of a bear attack. *Lie flat on your stomach. Don't scream. Try not to panic.*

Most bears would leave you alone after a few swipes, bored by the lack of fun.

Unless the bear already saw you as food.

Sadie had no intention of lying passively waiting for death. She flung herself toward her gun, arms outstretched, but it had been flung too far away. The bear snarled and raced toward her, its teeth bared. Sadie closed her eyes and braced herself for the impact, knowing that she was out of options.

The impact didn't come. Instead, she heard a hiss and the bear snarling, and sat up to see Rick a few feet behind, aiming a can of bear spray at the beast. The bear backed away down the path, but it only seemed more agitated. Rick sprayed it again before aiming his rifle.

Sadie scrambled for her gun, her heartbeat pounding in her ears as she took in huge gulps of breath.

The bear backed away further before turning and lumbering off, heading up the gorge and disappearing into the trees at the bottom of the mountain.

Rick rushed to Sadie's side and reached a hand down to help her up, his eyes wide with concern. As he pulled her to her feet Sadie tripped and he caught her.

She looked up, straight into his face, and she was suddenly acutely aware of just how close they were standing. His eyes burned into hers and his soft, full lips were just inches away from her own.

His gaze dropped to her own mouth and Sadie's whole body quivered with anticipation as for one crazy moment she thought that he was about to kiss her.

Even crazier was the fact that she wanted him to kiss her.

Rick's eyes had gone dark with unmistakable desire, and his hands, which were still on her waist where he had steadied her when she tripped, applied gentle pressure to pull her further into him. Sadie held her breath.

Then Rick stepped away.

He looked away, giving an embarrassed cough, and Sadie quickly changed her own stance, replacing her gun in its holster with shaking hands.

"You should get those scratches on your neck seen to."

Sadie touched her neck, where her scarf had unwound and the bear's claws had caught her. She was bleeding and hadn't even noticed.

What the hell just happened?

"Thank you," she said in a shaky voice. "I think you just saved my life."

"Thank God I came across you," he said, his brow creased. "Why are you out here on your own? And with no bear spray?"

Sadie swallowed, searching for an answer. "Carson asked me to fetch something from his cabin for him," she said at last, knowing it sounded lame. "He can't leave the hunt; he's helping to lead it. Anyway, I could ask you the same thing," she challenged.

"I'm a zoologist," he said reasonably. "I'm often in the wild on my own. I wouldn't recommend it to anyone who doesn't know what they're doing. Especially with a manhunter on the loose."

"I'm not some urbanite," Sadie snapped. "I was born and raised around here."

Rick just looked at her, his eyes searching, and Sadie felt bad for snapping at him. He had just saved her life. But the near kiss and her moment of vulnerability had left her feeling agitated and unnerved.

"Do you think that was the bear who killed the women?" she asked in a friendlier tone.

"I think so," Rick said, "although I still have some prints to check. You were lucky; you could have been dinner."

Sadie shuddered at the thought. So much for bears being cuddly.

"I've never been so scared," she admitted. "I've faced down some of the scariest killers imaginable, but a wild animal…that was something else. There's no motivation to work out, no potential for reasoning or negotiating…it just wants to get you and that's it. This is a brave job you do."

Rick smiled. "I could say the same about you. I would much rather deal with bears than some psychopath. Animals aren't evil; they're just doing what they need to do."

Their eyes locked again as though in some kind of shared understanding, and Sadie felt a jolt of surprise as she realized that it wasn't just that she was attracted to this man, she actually *liked* him. There hadn't been many men that she could say that about.

Not Sheriff Cooper? Caz's voice asked inside her head. Sadie shut that thought straight down. This was no time to be thinking about the weird, unspoken tension that existed between her and the sheriff.

Especially not when she had just been moments away from kissing another guy.

Sadie coughed, giving herself a mental shake. "Right. I suppose I had better do what I came here to do," she said, motioning at the cabin.

"I'll wait for you," Rick said. "Just in case that grizzly comes back."

Sadie walked toward the cabin, glancing back over her shoulder at him. "Thank you," she said again. "I owe you one."

"In that case," Rick said with a grin that made his eyes crinkle adorably at the sides, "how about you let me take you for a drink sometime?"

Sadie froze as Rick waited for an answer.

A hundred reasons to say no raced through Sadie's head. She didn't want to complicate the case. She barely knew him. She was in no position, emotionally or practically, to start dating. People would talk. Caz would never shut up about it. The sheriff would be pissed.

But she didn't say no. "Why not," she said instead, her voice deliberately casual. Rick's grin widened and Sadie swiftly turned away and went into the cabin, not feeling casual at all. She tried to tell herself that she was just in shock. After all, she was almost mauled to death by a bear; of course her reactions were off. She would never usually contemplate dating—much less kissing—a colleague.

But he wasn't really a colleague, she reasoned with herself. Neither did a drink necessarily qualify as a date. Maybe he was just being friendly, and she had imagined the whole near kissing thing.

But that look in Rick's eyes as he had stared down at her, that had been naked lust…out of practice or not, Sadie was damn sure that she hadn't imagined that.

Enough, she reprimanded herself as she looked around, her eyes adjusting to the gloom of the cabin. *You're here for a reason.* She needed to search the cabin before Carson and the hunt came up this way on the trail of the bear.

As she stepped further inside the cabin the smell of long dead carcasses and musty pelts hit her. As well as the expected pelts hanging from the ceiling it looked as though Carson had been doing a spot of taxidermy as well. A fox's head stared at her from a table, fixing her with its glass eyes. Next to it, a raccoon was forever poised to leap, its little claws curving in the air.

In the half-light the shadows looked bigger and the stuffed animals almost real. Trapping and taxidermy were hardly rare in Alaska, and stuffed animals made good sales to tourists, but nevertheless there was something about the practice that left Sadie cold, making her wonder what type of person could happily do that work without finding it gruesome.

It seemed creepy to her, and maybe it was a far-flung correlation but Carson, too, had struck her as creepy even before Sadie had caught him replacing Jane Winters's panties. She thought about the accepted wisdom that psychopaths—especially tormentors of women and girls—often showed a propensity in childhood for hurting or even killing animals. Did an interest in taxidermy count?

Steeling herself against what she might find, Sadie began to search a wooden desk that ran the whole back length of the cabin. She squinted at the main item that was on the top. It was a large bear's paw, waiting to be worked on as the sinew and bone were still showing at the wrist. It had been a big bear. Sadie wondered if there was much call for stuffed bear paws.

Unless that wasn't what it was for. Her mind raced as she ran through the possibilities. Could Carson be using it to plant bear tracks? Perhaps the women weren't killed by bears at all? Pete had identified the teeth marks in the bodies, but could Carson have staged those with a jawbone or similar? She wasn't a forensic expert, but it had to be possible. And Pete had only made a cursory exam of the bodies because they weren't supposed to be murder victims.

She wanted to call Rick inside, to see if he could match the bear paw to the tracks and ask him about her theory, but she knew that she couldn't get him involved. Not while she was investigating this in a completely unofficial capacity. If she could get a case open, it would be a different story.

Sadie pulled open a small drawer under the desk, hoping there was more to find. Enough evidence to finally call the case what it was and bring Carson in formally for questioning.

And there it was.

A woman's hairbrush, with a tangle of hair caught in it. Hair that looked to be the same color and length as Marie DuVale's. Next to it lay a crumpled pair of lace panties. Vastly different from Jane Winters's plain cotton briefs, this was a lace thong that Sadie could imagine being the choice of the more flamboyant DuVale.

Sadie quickly bagged the items and decided that she would head straight back to the station and ask Pete to have a look at them. Pete was good at not asking questions or offering opinions that he hadn't been asked for, and she knew she could trust him to do as he was asked without broadcasting it around that the bear kills might not be quite what they seemed.

Sadie walked back outside, avoiding the swinging pelts. Rick was waiting, his hands in his pockets as he stared out across the mountains. He looked lost in thought but turned as soon as he heard Sadie.

"Got what you needed?" he asked.

"Yes," Sadie said. "I had better get back."

Rick frowned. "How will you know where the hunt is?" he asked, and Sadie knew that he must be aware that her flimsy excuse for being here was just that. If he thought so though, he didn't ask, much like Pete.

"I'm meeting Carson later," Sadie said smoothly. "I'll head back to my truck now, it's not too far."

"I'll walk you back," Rick insisted and although Sadie wouldn't have admitted it, she was relieved at the offer. She had no desire to go trekking around on her own again knowing that the manhunting bear was still out there somewhere. Not to mention the rest of the animals that they had seen up by the river. Her legs felt badly bruised now from where the bear had sent her flying to the ground, and the side of her head pounded where it had hit a rock. She would be black and blue tomorrow.

They fell into step alongside each other and walked across the ice and back to the main pine woods. The snow was deep and crunchy underfoot and a hushed silence seemed to fall across the landscape.

"You were lucky to grow up around here," Rick said after a while. "It's so beautiful and unspoiled. The tundra teems with wildlife too, even if people don't always notice it."

"It is beautiful," Sadie agreed, "but it is also treacherous." She thought of Jessica. "My sister drowned in one of the frozen lakes." She omitted the fact that she didn't believe it was the ice that had killed her. Usually, she didn't mention her sister to people at all, much less a man that she had only just met. There was something about Rick, though, made Sadie want to confide in him.

He turned his head swiftly. "My God, I'm sorry, Sadie."

"It's okay," she said awkwardly, wishing she hadn't said anything. "I just meant that it can be as deadly around here as it can be beautiful."

"It certainly isn't a place that seems made for civilization," Rick said after a pause. She felt relieved that he had picked up on her reticence to talk about Jessica and not pursued the topic.

They reached her truck and she said goodbye, wondering—or maybe even hoping—if he was going to mention taking her for a drink again. But he only raised a hand awkwardly in a wave and watched as she clambered into the driver's seat. She looked back and their eyes met again, and Sadie felt that jolt of connection, an unspoken mutual awareness of each other.

As she drove away, she fought the urge to look back at him in her mirror and kept her eyes resolutely on the trail in front of her. There was no time to moon around after a man, however easy on the eyes he might happen to be. She wanted to get back to the station before Pete left for the day.

It would be dark soon and the sheriff would be back from the hunt. Sadie hoped she could convince him to agree to bring Carson in for questioning. They might just be about to get somewhere.

She thought about the bear paw again and whether or not her earlier theory was even possible. But the thought only brought her mind straight back to Rick, because she couldn't help thinking how upset he would be if the bear was killed when in fact it wasn't a maneater at all. It couldn't be the case, she thought; surely nothing but teeth and claws could make that kind of mess, but she also knew how ingenious people could be when they wanted to get away with murder.

Which was why she needed to be on point if she was going to crack this thing, not distracted by a potential fling.

She was arguing mentally with herself all the way back to the station, telling herself that she deserved some fun in her otherwise serious and intense life, at the same time as her more typical, cautious side warned against it. People were being killed and her father was in the hospital. They were her priorities.

Before there were any more deaths.

65

CHAPTER THIRTEEN

Back at the station, Sadie waited as Pete examined the hair in the brush.

"You'll have to wait for DNA results from the lab," he said, "but the hair certainly seems to match Marie DuVale's. The panties are similar to the ones she was wearing when she was attacked; they could be part of a set. So it's a good bet that they were hers."

"Thank you," Sadie said, taking the items from him and bagging and tagging them to go to the lab. She was hoping she wouldn't get hauled over the coals for wasting money, because technically there was no murder investigation to be collecting evidence for. A lonely trapper stealing dead women's underwear was gross, but it hardly warranted a forensic investigation.

She needed concrete evidence that the bear attacks were staged. Otherwise, Golightly would be pulling her back down to the Anchorage field office and she would get no chance to investigate further. The thought of leaving the case unsettled galled her.

It was too close to home. Jessica's death had been ruled as inconclusive and the case closed, leaving Sadie still trying to get justice all these years later. She didn't want to see the same thing happen to these women.

As she made her way back up to the reception area, Sheriff Cooper came through the doors, covered in snow and looking tired. By the expression on his face, Sadie guessed that the hunt had been unsuccessful.

"Nothing?" she asked.

"We got some hits with the dogs," Cooper told her, looking frustrated. "But after hours chasing the scent, we lost it up near the widest part of the river. We didn't come across one bear. It's as though they've vanished. I wouldn't be surprised," he muttered darkly, "if Bonsor did something to make them leave the area so that we don't kill any of them."

"I know you don't like him," Sadie said, "but I don't think that's true. I nearly got attacked by a bear on the way to Carson's cabin. I think it was tracking me. I was lucky that Rick turned up and used his bear spray on it. He could have saved my life. He's trying to help, Cooper," she reprimanded softly.

"Right," Cooper said shortly, sounding less than impressed. "So, when you sneaked off to search Carson's place—which I advised you not to do—you nearly got yourself killed, that's what you're telling me?" His eyes fell to her neck and widened. Her scarf had slipped, and she guessed the scratches from the bear were clearly visible. She had applied antiseptic as soon as she had arrived at the station, but Rick was right; she really should get them looked at.

"I'm fine," she said before Cooper could ask.

For a moment they both stood, staring at each other. Sadie had rarely seen the sheriff so riled as he was lately. Although he appeared as collected as ever, she could see the pulse throbbing in his jaw, a sure sign that he was upset.

"Carson may have stolen items from DuVale as well as Winters," she said eventually, her tone clipped. This wasn't the time to address Cooper's obvious issue with Rick. "I found a hairbrush and another pair of panties in his cabin. The hair matches DuVale's and the panties are similar to the ones on her body. I'm sending them to the lab to confirm." She raised her chin and looked at him defiantly, waiting for her to argue with her about wasting resources. This was his jurisdiction, after all, and she wasn't officially part of this case.

Instead, Cooper walked past her and sat down heavily in the battered wooden chair behind the reception desk. Like everything else in the station, it was old and dusty. Very different from the FBI field office, which was a lot more modern and definitely better funded.

She wondered if, deep down, Cooper still resented her presence on his turf. If at some level, she would always be a female version of Rick to him; a useful colleague, yes, but also just another out-of-towner throwing their professional weight around. Even though she was a local, and Cooper was born and bred in Juneau, not Anchorage, he was the one who seemed more at home here now, whereas Sadie felt like the outsider.

"So, he was sexually obsessed with both victims," Cooper said instead. "Leaving aside the way the women were killed for a moment, is it likely for a man like that to escalate to killing them?"

Sadie took the chair opposite him. This was territory that she was more familiar with, her own area of expertise.

"Yes. In fact, it's more likely than most people would anticipate," she said, drawing her knees up under her. She felt suddenly chilled to the bone even though it was relatively warm in the station, and she wondered if shock from her near miss with the bear was setting in. "We tend to see such behavior as creepy and suspect that maybe it can eventually lead to violence, but often we would view a guy stealing women's panties as just a bit of a pervert. Yet stalking and sexually obsessive behavior is identified in the majority of criminal homicides."

Cooper's eyebrows shot up his forehead. "Really?"

"Yes. Killers often choose their victims ahead of time, and there can be a build-up to the act itself, particularly if it is sexually motivated. They fantasize, watch the victim from a distance, and then make efforts to get close to them. Taking trophies like panties and hairbrushes is quite far along that process. He's forging a physical link with them, in his mind. It's almost like foreplay."

The sheriff visibly shuddered. "And the murder itself...is the consummation."

"Exactly." Sadie nodded. "But that's where things become unusual...bear attacks? It's too impersonal. Unless, as we said earlier, the point of the bear attacks was to cover up evidence on the bodies themselves. Bodies that are torn to shreds by animals won't be examined for proof of sexual assault, for example."

Cooper leaned back in his chair, staring at the ceiling as he exhaled through pursed lips.

"It makes a horrid kind of sense," he admitted. "And while it might seem bizarre to me, for someone like Carson who spent most of his life around the woods and the bears, it could be the perfect murder."

There was another pause as they both contemplated the implications of this new theory. But was Carson really capable of pulling off such a plot? Sadie wasn't so sure.

"I don't know Bobby Carson," she said. "Does he have any priors? Any stalking or sex offenses?"

"I'll check the database, but I'm not aware of any. What he does have," Cooper said grimly, "is convictions of battery against his ex-wife. I'm the one who arrested him. Three times. So he's not a stranger to violence against women."

"If the lab comes back conclusive for the items, we have good enough reason to bring him in," Sadie said. "We could open a formal investigation then."

"Yes," Cooper agreed. "But I don't want to wait until then to question him." Cooper stood up and started zipping his coat back up.

"You don't?" Sadie was surprised.

"When we disbanded the hunt for the day and left him," Cooper explained, "one of the men offered him a lift back to his actual residence, up by the Native village. But Carson said he was going to his trapper's cabin. I was worried, then, that he would catch you around there. But now, if he goes back and sees the items are gone and he knows you could have spotted him returning the underwear at Winters's place this morning…"

"He might make a break for it," Sadie concluded, standing up herself.

Any tension between them was gone—for now at least—as they headed back out of the station to go and question Bobby Carson.

*

They drove the last part of the way up to the headwaters with the lights off, trying not to alert Carson, or any lingering bears, to their presence.

"We'll park up here and go the rest of the way on foot," the sheriff said, bringing the snowcat to a stop. As they stepped out, Sadie heard a howling coming from the mountains and the cry of an owl overhead. It was already pitch-black, the darkest time of the year in Alaska, when the hours of sunlight were few.

It really was the perfect time of year for a murder, Sadie couldn't help thinking. She followed Cooper as he moved stealthily through the shadows toward the trapper's cabin, his hand hovering over the holster of his gun.

Sadie already had hers in her hand. If Carson was around, and still armed with that rifle of his, then they were at a disadvantage here, on his turf. He knew this part of the land better than either of them.

It was also dark enough for a bear to go unseen. The thought of being caught by a grizzly again made her heart pound faster in her chest. It was ironic, Sadie thought, that a wild animal was able to scare her far more than a potential serial killer. But she was used to dealing with serial killers.

And what the hell does that say about my life? she thought. Something was definitely wrong there.

As they approached the cabin, Cooper suddenly stopped dead in front of her.

"What is it?" Sadie hissed.

"It looks like the door is hanging off," Cooper whispered, taking out both his gun and his flashlight. In the small circle of light Sadie could see the wooden door was indeed hanging from its hinges, but it hadn't been neatly kicked open but rather was splintered and torn apart.

69

Sadie covered Cooper's back as he entered the cabin, then followed him.

She heard his shocked inhale just as the smell of fresh blood hit her.

Bracing herself for what she might be about to see, Sadie turned on her own flashlight and then stepped inside the cabin. She pressed her lips together, fighting the immediate urge to vomit.

They had found Carson, but he wouldn't be coming in for questioning.

Just like DuVale and Winters, Carson had been all but torn apart, and blood and gore were splattered around the cabin, looking somehow oddly at home amongst the carcasses and pelts that hung from the roof beams. Sadie felt something squish beneath her boot and stepped back, willing herself not to look down.

Cooper turned and looked at her in disbelieving shock. Neither of them had been expecting this.

"What the hell?"

Sadie had no response for the sheriff. Whatever Carson might have had to tell them, the bear had gotten to him first.

CHAPTER FOURTEEN

The moon was high in the sky and shining through the door of the cabin by the time Rick arrived. He looked visibly nauseous at the scene in front of him, even though Sadie, the sheriff, and Pete had cleaned up as best as they could. Sadie had wanted it to be treated as a crime scene, but Cooper had shaken his head in defeat.

"The only suspect here is the bear," he had said. "Let's call Bonsor. He's the bear behavior expert. We need to get this bastard hunted down for the last time."

Knowing that if Cooper was prepared to call Bonsor in then he really had admitted defeat, Sadie had nodded mutely, and gone to stand by the window until Rick arrived.

He looked crumpled, as though they had disturbed him turning in for an early night, but the look suited him. A five o'clock shadow enhanced his model-like cheekbones. Still, as he looked around the blood-strewn cabin, his easy confidence had gone, and he looked horrified. Sadie felt sorry for him. Most people weren't used to seeing this sort of mess.

"Sorry to drag you into this so late, Bonsor," Cooper said grudgingly, "but I wanted your opinion on the actual scene of the attack. This is three attacks in two days. I've never heard of anything like this."

Rick looked as shocked as they were. "You're right, Sheriff. This is unheard of. On average, bears kill two people a year in America, not two a day. This bear is killing humans by choice now, not for lack of other food."

"They do that?" Sadie asked. Funny how, in spite of growing up knowing how dangerous bears were, she still expected them to be a bit cuddly at heart. To only attack if starving or threatened.

"I've heard of it," Rick said, staring around at the cabin in a kind of horrified awe, "but I haven't come across it. Bears who have become habituated to the presence of humans can, conversely, become more likely to attack because they have lost their fear of us, and that can lead to us being seen as a convenient food source. There was a case in Kamchatka in Russia where a group of grizzlies attacked a bunch of geologists at a mining company and uh, actually ate the security guards."

"A group?" Cooper looked disbelieving. "They can do this in groups?"

"The worst attacks on humans by brown bears have actually been in groups," Rick said. His voice sounded strained, and as Sadie watched him, she could see that he seemed sad underneath his initial shock at the scene. More than sad; devastated, even. With his next words, she understood why.

"It's something I'm concerned about," he continued, running a hand through his longish hair. "I spent today making casts of the tracks of the bears I suspected and matching them to the attack scenes. I've matched them to the big grizzly that you came across today, Sadie. It isn't the male I first thought, but the mother of the adolescent cubs. I believe she is taking body parts back to her cubs and therefore the rest of the group will get the scent. Which means that others could start following her lead. We don't know exactly what drives the group hunting phenomenon, because it is so rare, but we're fairly sure it starts with just one bear deciding that humans taste rather good."

"We need you on the hunt tomorrow," Cooper said. "We need to get this bear now. Mother bear or not, I'm pretty sure those rules don't apply now?"

Rick nodded again, albeit reluctantly. "She needs to be taken down. But can we at least try to spare the cubs? They're big enough that they may try and attack if they are close."

"You'll have to speak to Garcia about that," Cooper said, although not without sympathy. "He's leading the hunt."

Rick's mouth curled with distaste at the mention of Garcia, a fact that Sadie noted with interest.

As Rick went outside to look for bear tracks in the snow, Cooper held Sadie's eyes with an expression that she couldn't read. Was he angry with her, or himself, for being led on what he now seemed to think was a wild goose chase?

But Sadie wasn't sure she was ready to admit defeat just yet. "This is all wrong, Cooper," she said quietly. "Carson knew about bears, and about bear mitigation strategies. He would have been careful."

"What is he going to do against a huge grizzly who likes killing humans?" Cooper retorted. Sadie pressed her lips together stubbornly.

"Rick saw what was presumably the same bear earlier. It was about to attack me, and he saw it off," she argued. "Okay, so Carson isn't a zoologist, but he's not ignorant either."

"But there were two of us," Rick said as he came back in. "Bears are quite risk averse. Carson was alone and it's dark."

Sadie said nothing, feeling outnumbered. Part of her wondered why she was clinging to this so stubbornly, when so far, every theory had fallen dramatically apart. Cooper was right; it was time to give it up.

"You've done the casts already?" the sheriff was asking Rick. The zoologist shook his head.

"No. I just wanted to let you know there were pastry crumbs outside in the snow. Which explains the attack. Carson got sloppy."

Sadie ignored the warning glance that Cooper gave her and walked outside to see for herself. Sure enough, under a pine tree there were a few pieces of pastry, as if something had been tossed there half-eaten. This time, though, it didn't look like a trail.

She heard footsteps crunching in the snow behind her.

"When Carson left, he was eating a cold pie," Cooper said. He sounded almost pitying, and that made Sadie furious. She didn't need anyone to feel sorry for her. She could cope with being wrong.

"It still makes no sense that he would just toss food on the ground around here," she argued, although her heart was no longer in it. Perhaps terrible coincidences did happen after all. People got careless, even when they should know better. Animals went loco. And FBI agents chased leads that were only dead ends.

"Okay," she conceded before Cooper could answer with another rebuttal, "you're right. There's nowhere to go from here other than hunt the bear down before we end up with a whole bunch of them attacking humans."

"Well, McAllister's resort plans would definitely be on hold then." Cooper grinned darkly, attempting to cheer her up. Sadie smiled and was about to respond when Rick walked up to them, his eyes on Sadie.

"Seeing as I've been called out at this ungodly hour, how about last orders at the saloon?" he suggested. "I heard the rest of the hunt went there. And Sadie," he said with a slow smile that, despite everything else, made her stomach flutter, "owes me a drink."

"Does she now," Cooper said in a tight voice, his expression suddenly closed and hard.

"For saving me from the bear earlier," Sadie said quickly, but Cooper had already turned and was walking back to the snowcat, his back rigid, leaving Sadie with Rick.

It seemed that she was going for that drink after all.

*

The saloon was noisy, full of the local hunters, who were banging their bottles and toasting their future success the next day with a tray of shots. Garcia was in the middle of them and looked almost as though he was holding court. Caz and Ron were run off their feet for once.

"Where's Jenny?" Sadie asked as they reached the bar. Caz looked from her to Rick and Sadie saw her friend suppress a smile.

"Staying at a friend's house. This group isn't showing any sign of quieting down. At this rate I'll be open all night."

Caz often kept the saloon open at all hours. Alaska at night could be busier than in the day, what with the night fishermen and the trappers.

After they got their drinks, Sadie headed to a booth in the corner rather than staying at her usual spot at the bar. She could sense the curious eyes of the locals on her and Rick.

As he slid into the booth next to her, sitting close enough that their thighs were touching, Sadie tried to convince herself to throw caution to the wind. She felt humiliated by Cooper's dismissal and as a result was even questioning her own state of mind. Was she so on the edge that she was seeing serial killers where none existed?

But she also felt a spark of rebellion. The case, as much as it had been one, was over and she would be back under Golightly's watch in a few days. She wouldn't see so much of the Coopers. Rick would no longer be any kind of a colleague. Why shouldn't she pursue the attraction between them and see where it went? She was still a red-blooded young woman.

"What's the deal with you and the sheriff?" Rick asked abruptly. "I'm not treading on his toes by bringing you for a drink?"

"What?" Sadie said, surprised.

"It's obvious he has a thing for you," Rick said. "I'm a guy; I can tell. He bristles like a porcupine any time I talk to you. And you're a beautiful woman, why wouldn't he have a crush?"

His compliment came easily to him, and Sadie cursed her reactive skin as she felt her cheeks blush and knew she had gone as red as a tomato. Thank God for the dim lights in the saloon.

"Er, thanks," she said awkwardly, "but I'm sure you're wrong."

"About you being beautiful?" Rick looked amused.

"About the sheriff," she said hurriedly. "We're just work colleagues, if you can even call it that. He's the sheriff, I'm FBI, but we've worked a few intense cases together that have put us both in danger. He's just very protective."

Rick shrugged. "If you say so. I just wanted to make sure I wasn't getting in the way."

"Not at all," Sadie said. She knocked her drink back and met his eyes, the burn of the whiskey making her bolder. "I'm a big girl; I can make my own decisions."

"I have to admit I'm kinda in awe of you," Rick said. "I mean, I've never met a federal agent before. And you know you're quite the local celebrity, right? Apparently, you caught some big killer before Christmas?"

The case was too recent and the memories too fresh for Sadie to want to talk about it. She stood up. "I need a refill," she said. "Do you want one? You bought these."

At the bar, Sadie was relieved that it was Ron who served her and not Caz. She knew her friend would have a barrage of questions for her. She hurried back to the booth with their drinks and on her way, she noticed Rick was looking at Billy Garcia with the same look of disdain that she had noticed earlier.

"You don't like him," she stated as she slid back into the booth.

Rick looked at her as though he was wondering how to answer.

"Are you coming on the hunt tomorrow?"

Sadie blinked at what seemed like a sudden change of topic.

"No," she said. "I have to get back to work soon and I still have some paperwork to file from that case before Christmas. I've already wasted time today, really. I'm sure you big boys don't need my help," she joked.

Rick looked serious. "I was kind of hoping you would come along," he said, his voice low, "to keep an eye on Garcia."

Sadie frowned. "What do you mean?"

"I've worked alongside him a few times," Rick murmured, avoiding looking in the direction of Garcia and his hangers-on. "We are often at opposite sides of a conversation because our roles are quite different, but that's not why you will have picked up that I don't like him. It's more a case of not trusting him."

Sadie felt her instincts prickle, even though she told herself to stop it. *This isn't my case. There isn't even a case,* she reminded herself firmly.

"Not trusting him in what way?"

"Game and Wildlife includes areas that often conflict with each other," he said, taking a long swig of his drink before continuing. "There is wildlife conservation and behavior, which is where I come in as a zoologist, and then there's managing opportunities for the hunting and trapping of wildlife. That's Garcia's area. While I don't like—in fact, I hate—killing animals for the sake of it, I do understand that it is a big traditional pastime around here. And often a community building event. And of course, it brings in a lot of tourism money."

"Okay," Sadie said slowly, "so what's your issue with Garcia? Is it personal?"

Rick shook his head. "No. He isn't someone that I would want to get to know," he said shortly. "He heads up the hunting and trapping division, right, so of course you would expect him to be into those things, but..." He stopped talking and looked over at Garcia, who was loudly telling some hunting story to the enraptured locals.

"But..." Sadie prompted. She thought Rick seemed almost scared of Garcia, and that intrigued her, because he didn't strike her as a guy who would be easily scared.

"There's something *dark* about him, Sadie," he confided. "Like, he takes a pleasure in hunting that just isn't normal, and I've been around a lot of these guys. I'm not just talking about the thrill of the chase. There's something sadistic about him." He looked warily at her. "You think I'm crazy, right?"

"Not at all," Sadie said swiftly. "I believe instincts like those are important. We evolved them for a reason...to stay away from predators."

Rick looked relieved. "Yes, that's exactly how I feel around him. As though he's dangerous, somehow. I've heard rumors..." He shook his head. "I shouldn't be talking to you like this. But you have access to information. You would know if he had any kind of record?"

"I can look him up," Sadie said. "But what is it you think I might find?"

Rick shrugged. "I don't know, maybe I'm just being silly. Animal cruelty, maybe? Violence? Possibly drugs. There are rumors that he takes a hell of a lot of cocaine. I don't really know. I'm just worried about him being assigned to this. There are young bears involved and I wouldn't put it past him to try and take them down, too."

"It's illegal," Sadie pointed out, but Rick shook his head.

"They're adolescents, not really cubs. And if they were to attack to protect their mother..." He stopped talking and took another swig of his drink. "You must think I'm insane," he murmured, looking suddenly shy. "Going on about the bears like this."

"Actually," Sadie said honestly, "I think it's pretty inspiring how passionate you are. I like that."

"Do you?" He held her eyes with that same look that had passed between them when they had been about to kiss. Aware of the crowd around them, Sadie looked away, although she didn't want to.

"I'll tell you what," she said, "I'll come tomorrow and watch Garcia, okay? But I'll come as a local, not as an FBI agent. There's no need for a Fed to be on a bear hunt."

Rick looked relieved. "Thank you, Sadie."

Sadie stood up, wondering what she was getting herself into for the next day. "In that case I need to go and get some sleep. The hunt will be setting out at first light. This group in here will be nursing sore heads."

Rick smiled. "Can I walk you back anywhere?"

"I live just around back," Sadie said.

"Great," Rick said, getting to his own feet. "Then I don't have far to walk."

They headed out of the saloon and Sadie walked around to the back door to go upstairs to her room. Rick walked beside her in companionable silence and once again, Sadie was struck by just how easy she found his company to be. As she reached the door she hesitated.

"Well, I'll see you in the morning," she said. "Thanks for the drink."

Rick leaned in and, before Sadie could react, ever so softly brushed his lips against hers. Warmth flooded her whole body as he pulled back, gazing into her eyes.

"See you tomorrow, Sadie," he said and walked away.

Sadie watched him go, her fingers pressed to her lips. They tingled with the memory of his touch.

She had to wonder if it wasn't she who was in danger of being caught.

CHAPTER FIFTEEN

He waited for the lights in the cabin to go off and knew that the woman was in bed. She was getting on a bit and was a late sleeper and early riser, which meant his timing had to be impeccable. Some new tactics may be needed. As much as he hated to admit it—because he despised being wrong, or admitting to weakness—he had made too many mistakes so far.

He couldn't afford to make any more.

These were delicate operations. He could almost congratulate himself on his own cleverness in thinking up this whole scheme in the first place, if it wasn't for that sharp-eyed Fed who seemed to be hanging around the victims' cabins. She noticed too much and asked too many questions. She had no business being here, and her presence was an anomaly that he hadn't planned for.

Maybe he would have to take her out, too. It didn't seem as though she had much experience with wildlife, so it shouldn't be too difficult to stage some kind of accident.

But first, this one. The cabin was in a prime position, and the woman who lived in it seemed proud of the place. He had watched her earlier from the trees, painting the fence on the porch. She had looked up once, scanning the woods with a worried expression, and he had wondered if she could somehow sense him watching her even though he was expertly hidden.

Or maybe she was just being cautious, having listened to the news of the bear attacks on the radio. A lot of the locals who lived out here, or people who had been staying in the area, had already vacated. A couple of the guys had joined the hunt, which annoyed him, because they were clearly amateurs.

Most of them were, in fact. They only slowed the hunt down. You had to *know* bears to be good at hunting them. To be able to think like them and see the landscape through their eyes.

To see the victims through their eyes. To the bears, the people that they killed were just food. People that they hurt were nothing but a nuisance that had gotten in their way or, occasionally, were perceived as a threat. There was no malice in bears. They just were.

Although, when he had hung around to watch the kills through his binoculars, the spectacles of violence had thrilled him with their brutality. It was hard not to watch a huge grizzly tearing through flesh and bone with gusto and not speculate that, on some level, they were enjoying what they were doing. Just as a human hunter felt the thrill and adrenaline of the hunt and the final catch, an intelligent mammal like a bear, designed by nature to be one of the fiercest of predators, surely must revel in its own strength. Its own wildness.

He had almost felt sorry for the victims, watching those powerful jaws and deadly teeth tear them apart while they were still alive, but only almost. They were nobodies, really. Unimportant in the grand scheme of things. Just people who were in the wrong place at the wrong time.

Like this one, puttering about without a care for the danger she was in. She deserved to die, really, just for being so stupid. If she had any sense she would have gotten out of the area after news of the first attack, at least until the hunt was over. But no, she had stayed, and he was glad of her stupidity because it would serve his plan well.

Once he was satisfied that his prospective victim was safely asleep, he turned his flashlight to dim and started to canvass the area just beyond the tree line. He had spotted bear tracks there earlier and he wanted to take a closer look.

As he came across what he was looking for he smiled to himself. Yes, the beasts had already come sniffing around. They had the taste for human flesh now and were doing his work for him.

Even so, he had to be careful. With the first two kills he had been overly confident and had never expected that anyone would notice anything out of the ordinary. Most people looked at an animal attack and saw just that. It didn't occur to people to look any harder. They just cleaned up the mess.

Then that Fed bitch had turned up, spotting things that he had missed, and she had knocked him off his carefully structured plan. That annoyed him. He liked to be in control and in charge, and yet there she was, like an ever-present pest. Looking over everything with those too-searching eyes. Distrustful of everything. Not soft and nurturing like women should be, but hard and brittle. He needed her away from all of this, before she blew it all apart. She encouraged the sheriff to be suspicious too, and that meant two people watching for anything that didn't quite add up.

This should have been easy. Effortless, even. Yes, he had been a little careless in places, but none of that would have mattered without her poking around.

The more he thought about it, the more that getting rid of her too seemed like a good idea.

The bears were getting hungrier. Why not treat them to an extra meal? A side of deep-fried federal agent?

He laughed to himself, amused by his own joke.

As winter progressed, food sources for the bears would start to run out. And now he had supplied them with an abundant new one that was no doubt a lot tastier to them than cold salmon. Of course, they didn't have the intellect to be grateful.

The kills were purely a means to end, nothing personal, but he had to admit that he was starting to enjoy himself. That it gave him a rush to see how effortlessly he could manipulate both animal and human. That the humans, in fact, were often dumber than the animals. He enjoyed the preparation, and then the hanging back to watch his plans come to fruition.

The kill. The ensuing panic. You could smell the fear in the air after attacks like these. You could smell it in the amateur hunters, underneath the excitement and adrenaline. But of course, excitement was only a few degrees away from fear.

In fact, he could feel the anticipation curling inside his stomach even now as he thought about the next one, coming sooner than he had expected. As he made his way back to the Jeep, he took one last look back at the woman's cabin. He sincerely hoped that she enjoyed her sleep.

It would be her last.

CHAPTER SIXTEEN

Sadie felt nervous as she drove to the base camp for the hunt, which was again at Jane Winters's cabin. In the cold light of day—or as much light as there ever was in an Alaskan winter—she didn't know quite how she felt about last night.

About the kiss between her and Rick.

If she could even call it that. It had been the barest and briefest of touches, and Sadie had been too shocked to react. Did that even count as a kiss at all, really? Perhaps he was just a touchy-feely sort of guy.

But the way he looked at her...Sadie was growing warm just thinking about it, and she wished it wasn't affecting her so much. Rick had asked her to attend the bear hunt for a reason—to watch Garcia, not to flirt with him. Yet she knew her adrenaline levels were surging with more than just the hope of finding a new lead.

The other reason she felt nervous was because she knew that Sheriff Cooper would want to know why she was there. He couldn't stop her, of course. She was a local and had come out of uniform, as a local wanting to join in the hunt. After all, she had seen the aftermath of the attacks and was as involved as any of them.

But she knew that Cooper wasn't going to buy that, not for one minute. She couldn't tell him what Rick had said about Garcia. He would dismiss it as hearsay. The way he had looked at her at Carson's cabin, with that mixture of pity and exasperation, had floored her. More than that, he would be angry with himself for listening to her against his better judgment.

Unless she had some concrete evidence of wrongdoing, or of anomalies at the scenes of the attacks, he wasn't going to listen to any more of her theories.

Sadie wasn't sure herself why she couldn't just drop it. Every lead she thought she had was a dead end. There was no evidence that these attacks were really any more than hungry grizzlies gone rogue. Yet she felt certain there was more going on here. Nothing about the idea of three people in the same area being so careless during bear season made any sense. Especially not Carson. Whatever else he had been, he was a trapper. He wouldn't have left crumbs on the ground, not after seeing the bodies of DuVale and Winters so recently. Not knowing there were killer bears in the vicinity.

No, something was going on, and Sadie was determined to find out what it was, whether Sheriff Cooper approved of it or not.

That was why she had deliberately set out early, so that she could reach Jane Winters's cabin before he or the rest of the hunt arrived.

She still had the keys, and she wanted to get a look at that journal.

Sadie let herself in, wrinkling her nose against the acrid scent of dried blood, and made her way to the bedroom desk where she had spied the journal. She lifted it out and started to flip through the pages.

At first, there wasn't much to see. Future lesson plans, long ramblings about missing her dead husband, and some accounts of the wildlife and weather. Then a few posts about Carson caught her eye.

Carson is always hanging around lately, she had written. *He has a look in his eye that makes me extremely uncomfortable, or am I just being a middle-aged old lady flattering herself? He seems to want to be helpful. Perhaps I'm being ungrateful.*

There were a few entries about Clarity, but nothing suspicious. Jane seemed to have decided that staying in the cabin on her own wasn't doing her any good but only prolonging her grief. She seemed happy to sell and was looking forward to moving in with her sister in Juneau.

Then another post about Carson. *I let him in for a drink yesterday, and now I'm sure that things are missing. That he was in my bedroom while I used the toilet. I won't be letting him in again.*

The next day: *Someone is watching me, I'm sure of it. Is it Carson?*

Then a week ago: *I was coming back from my daily walk when I saw a Jeep parked among the trees. There was a man in it watching the cabin, but I couldn't make out his features, except it wasn't Carson. He wouldn't be able to afford a Jeep like that anyway.*

Sadie flipped through the remaining pages, feeling her stomach sink as she read the woman's final entries. *I saw the Jeep again in the distance. Next time I'm just going to march right up and ask the guy what he wants. Maybe I should tell the sheriff.*

Sadie wished that she had. She put the journal back, feeling both sad for the woman and fired up with the determination to find the man in question. It couldn't be McAllister; he had no reason to watch Winters. He had been adamant that it hadn't been his tracks at her cabin yesterday morning. And while a wife's alibi wasn't the most reliable, it was something.

So, if it wasn't McAllister, that meant there was someone else watching Winters—or the area around her cabin—in the run up to her death.

Sadie heard vehicles pulling up outside the cabin and walked outside. The sheriff had arrived, with Garcia and a few of the hunters behind him.

The Game and Wildlife vehicle was a flashy new Jeep, Sadie noticed, and her eyes widened. Why hadn't she spotted that the day before?

Cooper looked puzzled as he spotted her.

"Price? Why are you here?"

"I was wondering that myself," Garcia said, flashing Sadie a none-too-friendly look. "Not the usual ladies' outing, is it?"

Sadie ignored him. She held the keys out to Cooper, who took them but looked no less puzzled. "You didn't need to come out this early."

"I thought I would tag along and see the outcome of it all," Sadie said. Cooper looked angry and was about to speak when Rick arrived. As he approached, the zoologist beamed at Sadie, and she couldn't stop herself from smiling back.

Cooper saw her smile and his own expression shut down instantly, his eyes becoming opaque.

"You came," Rick said. "I'm glad you did."

Cooper's eyebrows shot up his forehead. "You invited her?" he said to Rick, sounding the way he did when he was interrogating a suspect. "On the hunt?"

Sadie felt affronted by his sudden rudeness, as though she had no place being here. It was Cooper who had gotten her involved in the first place, inviting her to the scenes of the attacks. Now he was acting like she was some kind of thorn in his side, and she knew that if she took the time to think about it, she would feel hurt.

She had thought they were friends.

Rick, seemingly oblivious to the undercurrents, nodded. "Why not?" he replied amiably. "I thought it would be nice to have someone around who is on my wavelength."

Cooper looked as though he was contemplating throwing Rick to the bears with his bare hands. He seemed lost for words, and Sadie wished the ground would just open up and swallow her. Perhaps this was a bad idea after all.

"Nice setting for a date," Cooper hissed at last and then stomped off to stand by Garcia as the hunter started barking out orders. Rick looked at Sadie in bemusement.

"He really doesn't like me, does he?"

"I wouldn't worry about it too much," Sadie said, feeling shocked herself by the sheriff's behavior. "I don't think he likes me very much at the minute either." Did he really think so much less of her, just for going for a drink with a colleague?

Or perhaps he was still angry with her for floating the idea that the attacks were more than that. She couldn't tell him she was partly here because of the information that Rick had given her about Garcia, not when Cooper seemed convinced that Carson's death had proved that there was no chance of foul play.

Thinking about Garcia, she turned her attention to observing him as a way to avoid thinking about the situation with the sheriff. That was what she was here for, after all. She watched Garcia as the man gave his orders and continued to watch him as Rick stepped up next to him to relay his information on the mother bear he had narrowed down as the culprit and his worries about the rest of the group.

The mood of the rest of the group was grim, compared to the excitement of yesterday. The news about Carson had gotten around, and the danger was all too real to them now. Garcia, though, looked raring to go, bouncing on his heels with impatience. Rick was right about him, Sadie thought, he was enjoying this.

When Rick stressed the importance of doing their best to leave the bear's offspring unharmed, Garcia snorted in derision. The murmuring amongst the other men made it clear they sided with Garcia rather than Rick. The sheriff said nothing. In fact, he looked as though he would much rather be elsewhere and would be glad when the whole thing was over. Sadie caught his eye and tried to smile in sympathy, but Cooper looked quickly away, ignoring her.

As they all headed off into the trees, Rick walking beside Sadie this time while Cooper was at the front with Garcia, she noticed the sedative gun hanging over Garcia's shoulder along with his shotgun.

"Isn't that sort of cheating?" she asked, pointing to it. Rick half laughed, although it was a bitter rather than an amused sound.

"Oh, it's not for the hunt itself. Garcia wouldn't 'cheat,' as you put it. But one of us has to have one. We could come across an injured bear, or startle one. But I'm sure he would rather reach for his shotgun. This isn't just a job to him. He'll take as many bears down as he can get away with."

"You're really worried about those cubs," Sadie stated.

"That's why I'm here," Rick said. He was about to say something else when Sadie's phone rang. Assuming it would be the hospital, she snatched it up, feeling surprised when she saw that it was Pete. He was at the station early. Surely he couldn't still be working on Carson's body.

"Hello?" she answered the medical examiner.

"Sadie. I tried Cooper but he's not picking up. I need one of you to come down here. I found something on Carson's body that I think warrants further investigation."

Sadie looked at the hunt ahead and at Garcia's confident, arrogant stride. The sheriff was far ahead in the distance. She wouldn't reach him without running, and that would disrupt the hunt. The sheriff was right in that she didn't need to be here. But she could be useful at the station. "Now?"

"Yes," Pete said flatly. "I think Bobby Carson was murdered."

Sadie sucked in her breath sharply.

"I'll be right there."

CHAPTER SEVENTEEN

Sadie virtually ran through the doors of the station, her brain working overtime as she wondered just what Pete could have found. After ending their call, she had run to her truck after saying a swift goodbye to a disappointed Rick, promising to call him for an update soon. She had tried to call Cooper on the way, but as Pete had said, his cell was switched off.

Rick was the last thing on her mind right now. She could get back to her fledgling love life later.

Pete met her in the reception area, which was still deserted. He looked tired and she guessed that he had indeed been up all night. Waiting for results to corroborate his findings? Whatever he had found, he was certain about it, or he would never have called so early.

"Pete, what is it?" Sadie asked him. He took photographs from a file and laid them on a desk.

"It was hard to see at first, because the head and neck has been mauled as you can see," Pete said matter-of-factly, in an understatement about the mess that was left of Carson's face. "But see there, just under the headline at the back of the neck?"

Pete pointed to a spot in the picture and at first Sadie didn't know what he meant.

Then, as she leaned closer, she realized what he was referring to.

Two tiny, symmetrical pinpricks were visible at the back of Carson's neck, on a mercifully untouched patch of skin.

Sadie looked up and met Pete's eyes.

"Needle marks?" she asked.

Pete nodded. "He was injected. I ran toxicology labs—I've been up all night—and the results are clear. He had ketamine in his system."

Sadie felt shocked. She had wanted evidence for a murder, but now the full implications of it hit her.

"Ketamine, that's an anesthetic, right?"

Pete nodded. "It's a powerful tranquilizer. It incites extreme disassociation and a trancelike state. Under the influence you won't feel so much pain, but you won't be fully out of it as you would with, say, sleeping pills."

"So Carson wouldn't have felt much pain from the bear attack?" Sadie said, choosing her words carefully. Her heart was thudding in her chest as she tried to piece it together.

Carson had been drugged. Heavily. Which meant he would have been powerless to fight off the bear.

"Maybe not, but on the downside, he could have been aware of what was happening, but completely unable to move to get away," Pete said grimly.

Sadie felt sick. Carson had been a creep, but that was a godawful way to die.

And what about the women?

"Pete," she said urgently. "I need you to look over the bodies of DuVale and Winters again and see if there any needle marks on their bodies."

"You mean, what's left of them," Pete sighed. "They were more irreparably damaged than Carson. But I'll do my best."

"Can you run toxicology reports on them too?" she asked. If it turned out they had all been anaesthetized with ketamine before the attacks, then this was a serial killer case.

Sheriff Cooper would kick himself that he had missed it, but Sadie felt no satisfaction at this potential new revelation. Three people were dead, and if she couldn't work out who or why, then it may well not stop there.

"I can try," Pete said. "I'll let you know."

Sadie thanked him, and then frowned as something occurred to her. "Pete...was it a coincidence you noticed this or were you looking for anomalies in the body?"

Pete shrugged. "I'm not deaf. I've heard you and the sheriff muttering to each other. It isn't my job...but for what it's worth, Sadie, I'm with you. I think there's something off about this whole thing. Three attacks in two days? Something—or someone—is deliberately baiting this bear."

"Thank you," Sadie said quietly, feeling relieved that at least someone agreed with her.

"Are you going to tell the sheriff now?" Pete asked.

"He's at the hunt, so I'm struggling to reach him too, but yes, I'll try and catch up with him. He needs to know about this. I have another call I want to make first though; it could be useful."

She excused herself and went into Cooper's office, where she put a phone call through to the FBI field office in Anchorage.

Agent O'Hara answered, sounding pleased to hear from her. "Agent Price! When are we are going to see you around here? All everyone is talking about is that last case you solved."

O'Hara was a rookie on his first field assignment, and on the few occasions that Sadie had met him, she had gotten the impression that he had her on something of a pedestal. It wasn't something she wanted to encourage. People on pedestals had a tendency to fall off.

"I'll be checking in within the next couple of days," Sadie promised. "I haven't even sat at my new desk yet. Can you put me through to the ASAC, please?"

Paul Golightly, Anchorage's assistant special agent in charge, or ASAC, headed up the Anchorage field office and was therefore Sadie's boss. She liked him, but she also knew that he didn't suffer fools gladly and had no time for excuses. He was old school, and Sadie respected him for it.

"Price," he growled down the phone. "Where are you? You spend any more time in the hinterlands with that sheriff and you may as well become a local cop. I'm expecting you in this week. You have recovered from your hospital stay?"

"Yes, I'm ready to get back to work," Sadie assured him. "But I need just a couple of days. You've heard about the bear attacks?"

"I've heard that you saw fit to question George McAllister," Golightly said, and Sadie winced at his acerbic tone. So, McAllister hadn't been bluffing when he had said he knew the ASAC.

"He was seen driving away from the scene of the attack and he has an interest in the area," Sadie said in a neutral voice. "It was prudent to question him."

"Question who you want," Golightly said, surprising her. "McAllister is no more above the law than the rest of us. But what's the problem with the bear attacks?"

"Officially, nothing," Sadie admitted. "But something has come to light. There's an indication on at least one of the bodies that the bear may have had...assistance."

There was a brief silence at the other end of the line and Sadie braced herself for Golightly to scoff at the idea.

"When you say 'indication' what does that mean?" he said instead.

"Needle marks on the back of the neck," she told him. "The victim was sedated during the attack. I'm waiting for results on the other two. Sheriff Cooper doesn't know yet, he's out on the bear hunt. If the tox reports come back positive, then I need the go ahead to open a case."

She waited, trying not to think about how the sheriff would react if she opened up a federal case on this without so much as consulting him. Rivalry and even downright hostility between Feds and the local state troopers was common, and Cooper had initially been suspicious of her. His sister the deputy had been downright rude, although Sadie now considered her to be a friend.

But getting justice for the victims had to come first. That was her job.

"If you get positive tox reports, then sure," Golightly said. "Even if not, the evidence you currently have needs investigating. Is there any suspicion that the third attack could be different from the others?"

"Yes," Sadie said quickly. She filled him in on her initial suspicions of Carson and his obsession with DuVale and Winters.

"So, you were on your way to question him, and he turned up dead? Did anyone other than the sheriff know you suspected him?"

"No," Sadie said. Golightly hummed thoughtfully, mulling over what she was telling him.

"What's the motive?" he asked eventually.

"Honestly? I have no idea," she said with a sigh.

"Any suspects? Other than McAllister?"

"He's been ruled out," Sadie said, although she wouldn't put him out of mind, but she wasn't going to tell Golightly that when the land developer currently had an alibi and no motive. "So, nothing concrete but…maybe. That's one of the reasons I was calling. I wanted to check the database to see if there is anything on a Game and Wildlife expert named Garcia."

"I'll tell O'Hara to get on to it and get back to you," the boss promised. "Anything in particular you're looking for?"

"Drugs, possibly. General violence, especially against women," Sadie replied. "Animal cruelty as well," she added.

"Why?" Golightly questioned her. "Providing a bear with a series of good meals doesn't seem very cruel to me."

"Not even knowing that the bear would be hunted down and killed?" Sadie pointed out. *And Garcia is leading that hunt,* she thought to herself.

"Good point, Agent. Give me a minute and I'll speak to O'Hara. Keep me posted. It's an interesting case…did you know I was a prolific bear hunter myself, in my youth?" he added, sounding nostalgic.

"Er, no," Sadie said, thinking that it was an odd comment to make. She ended the call, relieved that Golightly had given her the go ahead to run with it, but also now feeling the urgency of building a case before anyone else was attacked.

Agent O'Hara sent her the file in minutes. Sadie downloaded it and printed it off. Grabbing a coffee from the station's tiny kitchen, she had just settled down to read through it when her phone rang.

It was the hospital.

"Ms. Price? I'm afraid your father's taken a turn. He's fading fast and we are not expecting him to last the night. You might want to come down."

Bear hunts, needle marks, and Garcia's file were forgotten. Her father was dying.

Sadie rushed out of the station.

CHAPTER EIGHTEEN

Sadie looked down at her father and then looked away again, blinking back sudden, hot tears. He looked sicker than ever, as though he had collapsed into himself in just the last day since she had seen him. She had no doubt that the doctor's judgment was correct.

Her father was about to die.

A nurse was at the other side of his bed, writing notes on her father's chart. Sadie coughed politely and the woman looked up. "Yes, honey?"

"Can I have a moment alone with my father, please?"

The nurse nodded, a look of practiced sympathy on her face, and cleared out of the room with the chart. Sadie sat down on the chair next to her father's bed, exhaling with a heavy sigh.

The air in the room felt thick, as though her father's illness settled over everything like a miasma. It felt harder to breathe. Or perhaps, Sadie thought, it was her and the weight of her memories. Hospitals reminded her of her mother's cancer and subsequent death, and now here she was back again with her father.

Except that this was different. She was an adult this time and was also alone. Jessica had gone too, and there would only be her left, the last surviving member of a wholly dysfunctional family. She wondered how Jessica would have coped with this, if it had been her sister who survived and Sadie who had drowned underneath the ice on a frozen lake.

Not drowned, she reminded herself, murdered.

She looked at her father and gave a bitter little laugh.

"I knew it would be too much to expect, Dad," she whispered to him even though she knew he couldn't hear her. "That you would actually come through for once. You couldn't have timed it better if you tried, you stubborn old bastard."

She felt a sudden, odd affection for him, lying there so helpless and yet somehow still managing to ruin her life. It was hard to remain bitter, though, when he looked so frail. Maybe this was what it took for the wounds between them to finally heal.

Sadie shook her head at the cruelty of life, but then whoever said that the world was fair? There would be no need for the job that she did if that was the case. All you could do was your bit to try and make things right, because to someone, somewhere, it mattered. To try and make sure that justice was done, even if it never really was done.

After all, catching killers couldn't give the victims their lives back.

And there was no bringing Jessica back. She could almost believe it was for the best that she would never know what really happened to her sister, but Sadie knew that she just wasn't made like that. The truth was important.

"What is it that you know, Dad?" she whispered. "What were you finally about to tell me?"

For a moment she had the sense that her father had heard her. His eyelashes flickered and the space between his eyebrows creased ever so slightly, and she leaned forward, excitement leaping in her chest as she wondered if he was about to wake up after all.

But there was nothing but the hum and rasp of the machines keeping her father alive. She had imagined it, or it had been an involuntary reflex. He couldn't hear her.

But the fact that he couldn't hear her meant that he couldn't argue with her either, and Sadie found herself talking to him about the case, using him as a sounding board for all of the things going through her mind.

Her dad had been a clever guy underneath all the alcohol. If they had been closer, Sade wondered if she would have spoken to him about her cases and asked for his opinion. Sometimes outsiders could give a fresh pair of eyes.

"Maybe you would see something I can't," she mused. "Because I can't get into the head of this killer. It's too bizarre and I've never come across anything like it. Why bears? What could anyone seek to gain from this? The best explanation that made any sense was McAllister, but he seems to be out of the running. Winters had signed the contract. There was no need to kill her. And Carson's trapper hut was outside of the resort area."

She shook her head in frustration. "It's a mess. I can see why the sheriff thinks I'm going crazy. Paranoid. Seeing killers everywhere. Maybe he's right, and maybe I do, but the tox reports? That ketamine in Carson's system is cold hard evidence that something is going on here. It changes everything. Carson didn't inject himself."

The old-fashioned clock on the wall chimed the hour, and Sadie looked up at it. The morning was getting on and the hunt would be in full swing. Both Rick and Cooper must be wondering where she had gone.

She should go back. There was nothing that she could do here, and she needed to get hold of Cooper as soon as he was done with the hunt so she could update him on the new evidence. But what if she left and then her father woke up?

It wasn't just about Jessica either, although the realization that she was feeling any empathy for the old bastard shocked her to the core.

She didn't want him to wake up and realize that he was alone. That she had left him to possibly die alone. Even if he would only tell her to go away if he knew she was here.

He was just an old man now. Not the ogre from her childhood, or the bitter old alcoholic mourning his favorite daughter and never missing a chance to tell Sadie that he would have preferred it to have been her body that was found. He was just an old, sick guy with no one, and the only flesh and blood that she had left.

Really, she was as pitiful as he was.

Sadie stood up, feeling restless. Sitting here was just making her feel pensive and morbid. She needed to be doing something. But what? She could rejoin the hunt, sure, but it wasn't the bear that she needed to catch. And she couldn't pull Cooper away from the hunt until it was over. She was on her own for the moment. Until she got the tox reports back for the women, however, there seemed to be little that she could do.

Those tox reports would be crucial because they could show a pattern to the deaths. Otherwise, it was only Carson's that could be ruled as suspicious, and the ketamine on its own wasn't enough. What tied ketamine to the attacks?

An image of Garcia striding ahead of the hunt earlier came to mind, and Sadie remembered her questions to Rick about the sedative gun that Garcia had been carrying.

What she didn't know was what sedative it contained, but she was sure that she had heard about ketamine being used as an animal tranquilizer.

Was it enough to knock out a bear?

Rick answered on the second ring, to her relief. In the middle of the hunt, the men were unlikely to be attending to their phones. She allowed herself to be flattered thinking that Rick had been waiting for her call.

"Sadie, is everything okay?"

"Yes. Listen," she said urgently, "that sedative gun of Garcia's. What sedative is in it?"

"Ketamine, most likely," Rick said, sounding confused. "That's what we usually use. Why?"

Sadie closed her eyes, mentally kicking herself for not thinking to ask as soon as Pete told her about Carson's tox report.

"I'll tell you later," she said vaguely. "Where are you guys? I'll come and meet you."

Rick told her they had just circled back around by Jane Winters' cabin. The hunt had been fruitless so far. It was as though the bears knew they were coming for them.

"I'll wait here for you," Rick said. "And then we can catch the others up."

Sadie left the hospital with one last, lingering look at her father. "Don't die on me," she said. "Wait until I get back, okay?"

The only answer was the drone of his breathing apparatus.

*

Rick met her outside the cabin with his usual charming smile in place, but Sadie was, for the moment at least, more interested in what he could tell her. She could admire him later.

"Where have you been? I was starting to think you weren't coming back." He said it in a light-hearted way, but Sadie saw the concern in his eyes. For a moment, it annoyed her. What was it with him and Cooper trying to take care of her lately? She could look after herself.

"Top-secret FBI business," she joked, but Rick didn't look any less worried.

"You were asking me about ketamine?"

"Yes, I was." Sadie paused, wondering how much to tell him. "I was thinking about what you were telling me about Garcia last night," she said, changing the subject slightly.

"I probably shouldn't have been so open with you about that," Rick said, looking uncomfortable, "But there is something about you that makes me forget you're FBI. It's easy to confide in you. That must be useful in the interrogation room." He smiled again and Sadie felt flattered that he felt that way. She was used to people feeling intimidated by her or wanting to pick a fight.

"I'm glad you were, honestly. I need your expert opinion. Does anything strike you as odd about these attacks? I mean, other than the fact that a bear killing a human is generally rare?"

Rick tipped his head to one side, looking lost in thought. Finally, he shook his head, looking confused. "Can you be more specific? What is it you're looking for?"

"Obviously, I'm not the bear expert," Sadie said, "but it seems weird to me that a bear would have to be really desperate for food to even start killing humans like this. Even if she is a mother bear. I know it's winter, but there were plenty of salmon in that river. Why would she go looking for more? I know Marie DuVale left food lying around, but why would the mama bear be sniffing around those cabins in the first place? It's so rare that they come that close." She paused, trying to make sense of her own train of thought without giving away her more sinister suspicions.

"What people forget about bears," Rick replied, "is that they play by their own rules. I can make good general predictions about grizzly behavior and nine times out of ten, I'll be right. But there is always that other one. You have to remember that bears aren't just the apex predator of Alaska but of the whole of North America. It's in their nature to kill, and sometimes they will do just that. We learn to co-exist with them, to use strategies to protect ourselves, and we even hunt them and think we are in the ones in control. We were lucky that the bear spray worked yesterday. But what human, alone and unarmed, could really stand a chance against a bear that had decided he was prey?" His eyes shone with passion as he talked about his favorite subject.

Sadie shuddered as she thought of her narrow escape the day before. She knew that better than anyone. She could so easily have been the grizzly's dinner.

Instead, it had killed Carson. But it hadn't been alone. Apex predator or not, no bear had injected the trapper with ketamine.

"I suppose what I'm asking," Sadie said, giving away as little about the case as she could, "is whether or not Garcia could be manipulating the situation? He seems just a little too keen to kill as many bears as possible. After the things you were telling me about him last night, I can't help wondering if he wouldn't try and engineer the final kill somehow."

"That's why you were asking about the ketamine?"

"Yes," Sadie said. It wasn't exactly a lie, after all. She couldn't tell Rick about Carson's body, not yet, but if she could get an official case open on the strength of the tox reports, she would be able to question him properly. He could be a particularly useful witness.

She couldn't help wondering how that would change the budding attraction between them. It didn't matter, she told herself. First and foremost, she was a federal agent. She had accepted the sacrifice of her personal life a long time ago.

Most of the time, she liked it that way.

"Like I told you earlier," Rick answered her, oblivious to her thoughts, "Garcia wouldn't 'cheat,' or at least not in an obvious way. He sees himself as this great hunter, so that would ruin his image. But am I worried he will take any chance to kill more bears than he needs to? Yes. That's why I asked you to come along."

"Okay," Sadie said. "We had better try and catch up with the hunt, then. Thank you for coming back for me. I know you want to be there when they catch the bear."

Just then, Rick's radio crackled and as he answered it, Sadie heard Sheriff Cooper at the other end.

"Bonsor. Where are you?"

"I came back to the Winters's cabin to meet back up with Sadie," Rick told him, and Sadie winced as she thought about how the sheriff was likely to understand that piece of news. "We're coming to meet back up with you now."

"Well, you need to hurry up," the disembodied voice of the sheriff told them, "because we've got the mother bear in our sights. She's with her cubs. And Garcia is baying for blood; he's whipped the rest of the men into a total frenzy. If you want to save the other bears, I need you here. I don't have the authority in this area to stop him."

"Where are you?"

"Back up by the gorge."

Rick ran, and Sadie ran after him.

She hoped she wasn't about to witness another murder. Only this one wouldn't be of a human.

CHAPTER NINETEEN

Rick ran slightly ahead of her, his long legs moving him easily through the woods. Sadie, who was a fast runner and could usually outpace most people, found herself sweating to keep up. They were at the gorge in no time, although her heart felt as though it was going to pound right out of her chest, and her body ached from the tussle with the bear the day before.

The first thing Sadie noticed as they reached the gorge was the atmosphere. There was an excited thrill in the air, an air of hungry anticipation, and it wasn't a pleasant feeling. Sadie felt her skin crawl as she saw the look of bloodlust on the faces of the men crowded around the gorge. She couldn't see what they were looking at, and as she tried to push her way through, she was shoved backwards.

"FBI," she snapped, pulling out her badge. Off duty or not, she always carried it with her. The man in front of her reluctantly stepped out of her way and she pushed forward with Rick close behind her.

Where was Sheriff Cooper? She looked around and saw him standing on top of an outcrop of rock, looking down at the river. His rifle was trained on its target and Sadie's eyes followed its trajectory to the headwaters of the river.

Just beyond the water, shaded by pines, were three bears, the mother and her cubs. Although cubs Sadie realized was a wholly inappropriate description of them. They were adolescents and, while not fully grown, were still big enough to do plenty of harm to an unarmed human.

The bears were feeding on something. Upwind, they weren't yet aware of the small crowd of humans crouched behind the rocks, observing them, or of the sheriff with his rifle trained down on them.

"Where's Garcia?" Rick murmured next to her with his voice full of worry. Sadie was thinking the same thing as she looked around for the Game and Wildlife hunter.

"I hope he's not trying to come around behind them," Rick said, shaking his head in exasperation. "He'll get himself killed."

"Surely, he wouldn't be so stupid?" Sadie asked. Rick snorted in derision. She doubted if the zoologist would think it much of a tragedy if Garcia did walk straight into the jaws of a hungry bear.

Although she couldn't see him going down without a fight, not if everything she had heard about him was true.

Then she saw Garcia, coming around the underside of the rock that Cooper was standing on, crouching so low he was practically in the water. He, too, had his rifle trained on the bears. He had gone straight for the bullets, Sadie realized, not for his sedative gun. Of course, the objective was to kill the mother bear before she could harm anyone else, but Sadie knew that had someone less bloodthirsty been involved, attempts would also have been made to disarm the younger bears without killing them. That was what conservation meant; not killing any more than necessary. No wonder Garcia and Rick clashed.

The look on the hunter's face was calm and focused, unaware of anything except the bears. There was a gleam in his eyes too that made Sadie shudder again. It was the echo of the bloodlust that she had sensed from the other men, but whereas for the rest of them this was a rare challenge, Garcia looked completely at home. He didn't look excited so much as entitled, she thought. As though this was his land, and they were his bears, and he would damn well do as he pleased with them. There was a narcissism in that which reminded her of the sicker serial killers that she had dealt with.

"I'm going to draw the mother bear out by taking out the largest youngster," Garcia said to no one in particular.

No!" Rick hissed. "The cubs are innocent. The hunt is for the mankiller only."

Garcia looked him up and down mockingly and then gave Rick a cruel smile.

"Still trying to save the animals, Bonsor? That cub is hardly innocent. Have you seen what it's eating? It's a human arm. Carson's, probably."

Rick raised his binoculars and trained them on the bears before lowering them, looking nauseous.

"That still doesn't give you the right to kill it," he protested. "It was the mother bear who killed Carson, not her young."

"How do you know her young weren't with her?" Garcia argued. "You can't rely too much on tracks in this weather. They're big enough to kill Bonsor; those beasts we're looking at are not furry little babies."

"It's illegal to kill the young ones," Rick protested, looking first at Sadie and then at Cooper for help. Sadie felt inadequate to respond. This was hardly her area of expertise. Unless Garcia went obviously too far, she had little jurisdiction to intervene.

The sheriff, too, looked torn. His eyes flickered briefly over Sadie and Rick, showing no emotion or recognition of the fact that they had arrived together. Then he looked at Garcia, frowning with worry, his brow creased deeply.

"He knows that's not true," Garcia said, jerking his head contemptuously toward Rick. "They're too old. They're not denning cubs, they're nearly full grown. And they are eating human flesh. You think they won't carry on killing humans after the mother is dead, Sheriff? Now that they have the taste for it?"

Rick looked almost like he was about to cry, his hands balling into fists at his side in frustration. Either cry, Sadie thought, or beat Garcia into the ground. Sadie looked up at the sheriff, who looked clearly out of his depth, his eyes flickering from Garcia to the bear and back again. In this situation, Rick and Garcia were the experts, and they clearly disagreed. Someone had to make the decision.

"We need to assess the risk," Cooper said carefully.

"There's no time for that," Garcia said angrily. "We've got all of them in our sights. We should kill them all now while we have the chance. Or there will be more killings, and the blood will be on your hands, Sheriff. That 'cub' is right in front of us, chewing on a goddam arm!"

Cooper looked sick at the thought and Sadie glared at Garcia, hating him for putting Cooper in this position, knowing that his first priority had to be the welfare of the townspeople.

Sadie wondered if it would sway his decision if he knew there was more to this than just bear attacks.

And what about Garcia? Did he know that? Did he know that she knew? The man raised his gun, oblivious to Sadie's suspicions, not prepared to wait for the go-ahead from the sheriff.

"No!" Rick yelled.

The mother bear heard them. From across the gorge, she looked over at them and snarled. Eleven rifles were immediately trained on her, and Sadie felt a tangible stab of sadness. She had to be killed but knowing what she did it felt bitterly unfair.

The larger cub snatched the arm that its sibling was feeding on and ran away back into the pines, spooked by the commotion. Garcia shot after it as it was fleeing but missed, the bullet flying into bark. A pine branch crashed to the ground and the two remaining bears roared in unison.

"You bastard!" Rick roared, running into the gorge toward Garcia, who swung his rifle on him.

"Stop!" Sadie yelled, drawing her own gun. "Rick, stay where you are! Garcia, get that gun out of his face or I'll shoot."

Garcia glared at her with such hatred that Sadie felt her skin prickle. He really didn't like her telling him what to do. Slowly, he swung his rifle back around to the bears.

Just then the other youngster came roaring toward them, teeth bared and ready to attack. Shots were fired simultaneously by the other hunters, but it was Garcia who got it, aiming his gun almost lazily, and Sadie watched as the young bear went crashing into the water, dead immediately from the well-aimed bullet to the side of its head.

Rick howled in despair and ran toward the body, kneeling next to it, his face as anguished as though he had just lost a loved one.

Sadie had the urge to go to him and comfort him, moved by the depth of despair on his face, but the mother bear, roaring in impotent rage at the death of her cub, was racing toward Garcia, moving so fast that she was almost a blur. No animal that size should be able to move so quickly, Sadie thought in awed wonder, momentarily frozen in horror as the scene seemed to play itself out in slow motion before her eyes.

From above, Cooper shot the mother bear in the flank, but it barely even slowed her down. The animal was moments away from reaching Garcia just as he was raising his rifle again, moments from taking him down to the ground with her powerful jaws to tear out his throat. She was leaping for him, and Sadie thought that there couldn't possibly be time to save him.

But then a volley of shots ensued, including one at point-blank range from Garcia. The bear reared back, went still for one horrible second with its face contorted in a last, desperate snarl, and then crashed to the ground. Blood sprayed everywhere, including all over Garcia who, Sadie realized, had barely flinched as the bear had come for him. He looked around at them, his face triumphant even though he was covered in blood, no trace of fear or shock in his expression. He wiped his hand across his face and then smiled down at it. It was covered in the bear's blood.

"I got her." Garcia grinned, as though the rest of the team had stood idly by while he was attacked. He looked down at the mother bear's body, and then across at where Rick was still crouching by the body of the younger bear, closing its eyes. He looked over at Garcia with such venom in his eyes it made Sadie flinch.

"Stop crying like a baby, Bonsor," Garcia mocked, unfazed by Rick's animosity. Perhaps even enjoying it, Sadie thought.

Garcia's eyes met Sadie's as though he had sensed her watching him. He seemed so pleased with himself, more than just the triumph of a successful hunt, and Sadie thought about the theory that had been taking shape ever since Pete had told her about the ketamine.

Garcia saw this whole situation, taking down a mankiller and her young, as some great achievement, maybe even the pinnacle of his career so far. Although he hadn't been alone on the hunt and it had been Rick who identified the guilty bear, Sadie knew that Garcia would take all the credit. He would receive it too, not just from the other hunters but from the local press. He would be the hero of the hour.

There must be a lot of kudos for a hunter, she thought, who was able to take down a rare maneater. Not many bear hunters could boast of that. And not just any maneater but one who had killed three humans in two days. It was an incredible story that would travel the whole of America and possibly even go international. Garcia would be a hero. Not only that, but Sadie suspected that the man experienced an almost sexual charge from the hunt and kill itself.

Could that, she wondered, be enough of a motive for him to stage the bear attacks?

To kill?

CHAPTER TWENTY

Sadie couldn't take her eyes off Garcia as he stood proudly over his kill as her theory took shape in her head and seemed to come alive right in front of her eyes.

Some of the local hunters were taking pictures of Garcia as though he was some kind of celebrity, while the bear and her young lay dead and vanquished near his feet.

There was something animal, certainly predatory, about Garcia himself, Sadie thought as she finally turned away in disgust, looking around for Rick. He was talking to the sheriff in a low voice, and Cooper for once was listening to him, while occasionally shooting disgusted glances at Garcia. Sadie approached the two men, hugging her arms around herself against an icy wind that had started blowing down from the mountains, as though the landscape itself was howling in protest.

They both looked up at her as she approached. Rick looked embarrassed, no doubt at his reaction to the death of the cub. As though compassion was a bad thing. She supposed that if you were a guy, surrounded by men like Garcia all day, then perhaps it was.

"That was ugly," the sheriff said. Sadie nodded. There was an awkward silence between the three of them before Cooper spoke again.

"At least that's an end to it now. The bears are dead, and the locals can sleep easy in their cabins again. It's finally all over."

Sadie said nothing. She needed to tell him about the ketamine in Carson's body as soon as possible, but she couldn't do that with Rick around. She was about to ask him if he was going back to the station precinct so that she could offer to accompany him when Rick spoke instead.

"Let's get out of here, Sadie. I'll walk you back to your truck."

Cooper's face immediately froze into the carefully shut down expression that he seemed to have adopted around her and Rick lately. He nodded brusquely at them both before walking off toward his own vehicle. Sadie jogged after him.

"Cooper, I need to talk to you," she said. He looked back at her as he was climbing into the snowcat. He looked exhausted, with purple shadows under his usually bright eyes.

"Now? Don't you have better things to do?" His eyes flicked back toward Rick and Sadie bit her lip to stop herself from retorting. She took a deep breath instead and spoke calmly.

"This is about work, Cooper, and it's important. Pete found something on Carson's body."

But the sheriff had already slammed the door and was starting the engine without looking at her. She didn't want to make a scene, not with both Rick and Garcia in the vicinity.

Fine. Sadie sighed to herself. She would have to go back to her truck, get rid of Rick, and then call the sheriff.

She walked back to Rick, trying to smile.

"Let's walk back, then," she said, at least glad to get away from the scene of the hunt. She glanced back at the dead bears. "What happens to the bodies?"

"Garcia will take them back to Game and Wildlife headquarters. His Jeep is big enough and the men can help him carry them. I've had enough of him for one day. I'll need to examine their bodies for traces of human flesh, just to make sure that we had the right bear."

"Is there any doubt?" Sadie asked, more rhetorically than anything else as she pictured the cub that had been chewing on Carson's arm.

"Well, no. But it needs to be evidenced. It isn't so different from what your forensics people do."

Sadie thought about that as they walked and concluded that Rick's job was entirely different from anything to do with hers. Perhaps, she mused, that was part of why she liked him. Although today had been tough, most of his job was about preserving life rather than hunting down killers.

As they walked through the pines back to Winters's cabin, Rick fell silent again, and she sensed that he was still feeling embarrassed.

Or guilty, perhaps.

"It's not your fault," she said. "You did everything you could to spare the younger bear."

"I didn't do anything," Rick said with surprising force and Sadie knew that he was right. He was blaming himself. But what could he have done? "I saw it coming... I should have tried to get Garcia taken off the hunt somehow."

"Would that even have been possible?"

Rick sighed so heavily it was more like a groan. "Maybe not," he admitted. "But I should have tried. I knew he was going to be a problem the minute he turned up. Still, like your sheriff said, it's over now."

Not for me, Sadie thought. She wanted to spend more time with Rick, to see how she felt after the kiss last night, but she had more pressing things to deal with first. She felt a little guilty, but right now she just wanted to get back to her truck so she could go after Cooper and fill him in on the new evidence.

So they could act on it before anyone else got killed.

They reached the cabin and her truck, and she stood awkwardly outside it for a moment. "Er, do you need a lift anywhere? Where's your Bronco?"

"I'm going to go for a walk, I think. Clear my head. Can I call you later?"

"Of course," she said softly. She watched him walk off into the pines, feeling oddly disappointed that he hadn't kissed her again, even though it wouldn't have been at all appropriate and there was no time today for romance.

She was climbing into her truck, still musing over her conflicting feelings, when Pete called her, and instantly Rick was forgotten as she snatched up her phone.

"Did you find anything?"

"Yes," Pete said, unfazed by her lack of proper greeting. "The tox reports for the first body, Marie DuVale, were inconclusive. But her body was a real mess. But Winters was a different matter. There was definitely ketamine in her system, and not a small amount either. And although she was ravaged, I can just make out what could be a needle mark on the back of her neck. Certainly, there's enough to tie both deaths together. In my opinion anyway," he said hurriedly. "Obviously, that part is your job."

"Pete, thank you," Sadie said sincerely. "Without your expertise, this case would be dead in the water. I haven't gotten the chance to tell Sheriff Cooper, but I'm going to call him now."

She ended the call, feeling her adrenaline rising. Now it was her turn to hunt.

She had a strong feeling that this time around it might be Garcia who was the prey.

Right on cue, as she drove carefully away from the cabin, Sadie spotted the Game and Wildlife Jeep. She frowned, realizing that Garcia was driving toward one of the holiday cabins. Had he rented one out? Or did he own one? The possibility that Garcia was more familiar with the surrounding landscape than she had realized was an interesting one.

To stage the attacks, the perpetrator would need to know the terrain well.

Thinking about the needle marks in poor Jane Winters's torn up neck, Sadie slowly followed him, hanging back enough that she hoped he wouldn't see her. When she saw him park in the distance and indeed head toward a small but smart wooden lodge, Sadie pulled up and phoned Cooper.

He answered instantly, his voice echoing. He was in the snowcat on his speakerphone.

"Sadie? What is it? Listen, I'm sorry I was short with you. It's been a long day and—"

"It doesn't matter," she cut him off. "Pete found ketamine in both Carson's and Winters's bodies," she told him without preamble. "DuVale's was inconclusive, but I would say it's a pretty safe bet it was given to her too."

"Sadie, what are you talking about? Hang on, let me pull over." He went quiet, then sounded closer as he put the phone to his ear.

"Say that again," he demanded. "You're saying they were both drugged?"

"They were unconscious—hopefully—at the time of the attacks," she said bluntly, then took a deep breath. "Cooper, I was right. The attacks were staged. The bodies have needle marks too. Pete wouldn't make a mistake like that. They were drugged."

Cooper was silent, and Sadie was tense, waiting for him to shoot her down again. Instead, he let out a long, low whistle.

"Son of a bitch. Any theories on who?"

"Garcia," she said instantly. "He has plenty of ketamine, Cooper, he's walking around with a sedative gun full of it."

"He has a cabin in the woods," Cooper told her, confirming her suspicions. "Assuming he's there and not at the saloon we'll go and speak to him. There's enough evidence to bring him in for questioning."

Sadie hesitated. "I'm already here," she said.

"Why does nothing you say surprise me anymore?" Cooper sounded long-suffering, but even that was a welcome relief from the cold treatment he had been giving her.

"Stay put," Cooper said when she confirmed she was safely in her truck. "Don't confront him on your own, Price. He could be dangerous."

"Cooper," she warned, "you're not—"

"Your boss, yeah, I know," he finished for her. "But for once, please, do as I ask?"

Sadie couldn't help but laugh. "Hurry up then," she said, and ended the phone call.

It took five minutes of tapping her fingers on the steering wheel before she reasoned that it couldn't hurt to have a look outside the cabin. Just in case there was anything incriminating, although she knew it was a long shot.

Moving carefully so she wouldn't be spotted if Garcia happened to look out a window at the wrong time, Sadie approached the cabin, her hand on the handle of her gun. There was no noise from inside the cabin and she wondered what Garcia was doing in there. Gloating, most likely, over his prestigious kill. She realized the bodies of the bears must still be in the back of his Jeep and wondered if they would reach Rick in one piece. She suspected Garcia would want a trophy of some kind.

A sudden stream of cold sunlight came dappling through the trees, shining directly onto Garcia's window, and Sadie was about to duck around the side of the cabin when she saw something inside gleaming in the shaft of sun.

The muzzle of a gun.

Sadie froze. Had Garcia spotted her after all, and was just waiting for her to come within range?

Or worse, did he have his next victim in there?

Whipping her gun out of the holster, Sadie approached the cabin door as the minutes seemed to tick by painfully slowly.

For once, she should have listened to Cooper.

She saw the gun flash again, and she placed her boot firmly in the center of the cabin door, mustering all her strength in one swift movement.

Just as she kicked it open, she heard the gunshot from inside the cabin.

CHAPTER TWENTY ONE

"Drop the weapon and put your hands in the air!" Sadie braced herself in the doorway, her gun in two hands, ready to shoot.

In front of her, a raccoon dropped to the ground from the window ledge. Garcia smirked, although she saw the fury flash in his eyes as he laid his gun beside him on the table.

"Agent Price," he said in a mocking tone. "Isn't that a bit of an overreaction for a raccoon?"

Sadie swallowed. She lowered her gun but didn't replace it into her holster.

"I heard a gunshot. That's the reaction I was trained to have." She raised an eyebrow at him. "Isn't a bullet an overreaction to a raccoon? You couldn't have just shooed it away?"

Garcia narrowed his eyes and Sadie got the impression that he was sizing her up. Then his gaze flickered up and down her body dismissively, as though he had decided that she was no threat to him. *Son of a bitch,* she thought, her fingers reflexing, curling tighter around her gun.

"What does it have to do with you what I do inside my own cabin? The last time I checked, it wasn't illegal to shoot raccoons. Wildlife is my jurisdiction, Agent, not yours. Why don't you run along and go and profile some pedophiles, or whatever it is that you do? Leave the big boys to get on with our jobs."

Sadie had never wanted to punch anybody quite so hard. Instead, she smiled at him sweetly.

"Does my presence threaten you, Garcia? Make you feel less of a man, maybe?"

Garcia snorted as though amused, but she could see the rage building inside him. A vein in his neck pulsed visibly and he drew his shoulders back as though deliberately showing off his heavy, muscled frame. His eyes looked wide with dilated pupils and his nostrils flared and Sadie realized that she recognized that look.

He was high. Her eyes went back to the table, noting a Visa card lying on its own near to where he had placed his gun. She was pretty sure that if she had it checked, there would be traces of cocaine on it.

"Don't flatter yourself, Agent," Garcia said, but she saw him notice the direction in which her eyes had traveled and she saw a hint of nervousness in his eyes.

Sadie didn't reply. She looked around the room casually, although she remained braced to raise her gun again if necessary. If he had recently snorted cocaine, he could be unpredictable. Violent, even. Especially if her presence started to make him paranoid.

But he could also trip himself up and confess unwittingly. She scanned the cabin, wondering what else he had to hide.

It was minimalist, with few home comforts. Spartan almost, which suited the tough guy image that Garcia seemed to want to project. Even if he only stayed here occasionally, she would expect at least comfy furniture, but there was only the table and a wooden chair. She wondered what the bedroom was like, thinking that she wouldn't be surprised if Garcia slept on the floor.

The walls, however, were a different story. Various hunting trophies adorned every spare inch, from Arctic foxes to moose, but most prominently, bears.

Garcia saw her looking and smirked again.

"I hope I get access to today's carcasses after the investigations are finished. A mother and cub would look great up there together, don't you think?"

"If you say so," Sadie said nonchalantly. "You were really pumped about the hunt today, huh?"

"I'm a good hunter," Garcia said proudly. "Unlike that boyfriend of yours, crying over a goddamn beast."

"He's not my boyfriend," Sadie snapped before she could stop herself, then inwardly cursed that she had allowed him to rile her.

"No?" Garcia was openly mocking her now. Sadie had met her fair share of assholes and chauvinists, but usually her badge afforded at least a modicum of respect, but not from this guy. He spoke to her as though she was playing dress-up. Any natural wariness he might have had about antagonizing a federal agent was no doubt numbed by the cocaine. "Maybe the sheriff, then? They both look at you like you're some piece of ass. I can't see the attraction, myself." He leered openly at her breasts. "A woman should have a bit of meat on her bones, if you know what I mean."

Sadie was weighing up the consequences of a well-aimed kick to Garcia's balls when he stepped toward her, deliberately slowly.

"Why," he said in a low, menacing voice, all trace of amusement gone, "are you here, Agent? What were you doing sneaking around outside my cabin?"

"I need to ask you a few questions," Sadie said. "As does Sheriff Cooper." She decided not to tell him that Cooper was on his way to joining them, sure that Garcia would take it as a sure sign that she needed the back-up against him. "I can accompany you down to the station."

"I'm not going anywhere near the damn station," he growled.

"Okay. How about the FBI office then?" Sadie said helpfully. She saw Garcia clench a hand into a fist at his side and almost willed him to try it, to give her an excuse to shoot. Not to kill, of course, only a defensive flesh wound, but enough to put a dent in that ego of his.

He didn't seem scared of her at all, or rather, of the fact that she was pointing a gun at his chest. The man truly seemed to think that he was invincible. Or, more likely, he just couldn't conceive of a woman getting the better of him.

"I'm not going anywhere with you," he snarled. "How dare you think that you can show up here and start ordering me around? You have no right to do that."

"Well, that's where you're wrong," Sadie said in a conversational tone, "because I happen to have this thing called a federal badge. Which means that actually, yes, I do."

Garcia stopped slowly advancing on her and stood with his hips wide and his arms crossed in front of his barrel chest. "You uppity bitch," he said. He seemed genuinely surprised that she wasn't responding to his attempts to intimidate her. "Unless you're arresting me for something, you can get the hell off my property."

This wasn't going well, Sadie reflected. If Garcia was guilty of anything, he was never going to confess it to her.

But if she made him angry enough, he might just slip up.

"You seem very defensive, Garcia," she mused. "It almost makes me think that you have something to hide."

"I have nothing to hide," he snapped, but his right eye twitched compulsively. Lying or nervous or both? "I had every right to shoot those bears. It was a bear hunt, Agent. That was kinda the point."

"Just how much did you want that hunt to happen, though?" Sadie asked him, looking him dead in the eyes. "Enough to engineer it, maybe? Help it along?"

"What are you talking about?"

Sadie eyed him. He seemed genuinely confused, but she didn't trust him one bit. Garcia was a narcissist, in her opinion, and they could be incredibly good liars. Especially when it came to maintaining their image.

She decided to change tack. "How well did you know Bobby Carson?" she asked. "Had you met him before this hunt?" Carson was a well-known trapper, and it would be odd if he and Garcia hadn't at least come across each other over the years.

Now Garcia looked wary. "What is this about?"

Sadie was about to ask him a question about the ketamine when Garcia took his chance. He feinted suddenly to the side and then when Sadie raised her gun in his direction pivoted back, knocking the gun from her hand with a sweep of his arm. He was even stronger than he looked, but more importantly, he was quicker than he looked too. As her gun clattered across the floor, Sadie realized that she had underestimated him.

It was time for that well-timed kick to the balls.

Garcia bellowed in pain as her boot made contact with his groin, but it didn't slow him down as much as Sadie had hoped. As she raced for her gun, she felt her limbs scream in protest at the sudden movement, still battered and bruised from yesterday's run-in with the bear.

He grabbed her around the waist before her hands could close around her pistol and shoved her angrily into the back wall of the cabin, with such force that she felt as though all the breath had left her body. As he pressed himself against her and went for her throat, Sadie wondered what the hell was taking Sheriff Cooper so long.

Garcia squeezed her throat and although she struggled, he had her pinned with his considerable weight. A rush of panic went through her as she realized that in this moment, he could all too easily kill her.

But then his ego got in the way. He leaned back slightly, relaxing his grip, so that he could look her up and down and leer at her. It gave her just a little wiggle room for her right hand if she timed it correctly.

"You ever wondered what a real man feels like, Agent?"

Sadie responded by jabbing him in both eyes, hard. He roared, his hands going to his face, and Sadie slipped out from his grasp and pivoted, giving him a hard back kick to his groin. She knew no man could take repeated blows to that delicate area, and as Garcia doubled over in pain, bringing his face almost level with hers, she drove the heel of her hand hard into his nose, hearing and feeling the satisfying crack of bone as it broke. Blood rushed everywhere.

But Garcia had no intention of giving up easily. He swung at her, narrowly missing her face, but pain and rage made him careless, and he stumbled slightly. Sadie saw her chance and kicked him again in the thigh, causing him to stumble further, and while she had him unbalanced, she grabbed his head in a forearm lock and used his own body weight to propel him straight into the cast-iron wood-burning stove.

He fell to the ground with the impact, grunting in pain, and Sadie swiftly knelt over his back to twist an arm behind him, one knee pushed up against the top of his spine. She was ready for him to try and throw him off, but Garcia was defeated. He lay on the floor moaning with pain and offered no resistance as she cuffed his hands behind him.

"Now you are under arrest," she panted. Her throat burned where he had tried to choke her, and she was sure that her scratches were bleeding again, too.

She was about to radio Cooper when she saw a man approach the open door of the cabin out of the corner of her eye. She whirled around, automatically bracing herself for another fight.

"Price? What the hell?"

Sheriff Cooper stood in the doorway, looking stunned.

CHAPTER TWENTY TWO

After the ambulance and a state trooper had arrived to accompany Garcia to the hospital, Sadie suggested that they search the cabin for further evidence that Garcia was indeed their killer.

Cooper looked bemused. "Great idea, Price, but before we do that, do you want to explain what the hell happened here? Garcia's going to need stitches and his nose and jaw reset. You're gonna have some paperwork to file on this one."

"He attacked me," Sadie told him. "Knocked the gun straight out of my hand. Then he tried to choke me. I think he might have been about to sexually assault me too."

"Well, he will regret that," Cooper said lightly, but his expression was dark as his eyes dropped to Sadie's throat. "He's bruised you," he said. "Those marks weren't there yesterday."

"He wasn't playing around," Sadie said. "At first, I think he was just trying to insult me, but when I told him we needed to ask him questions he went crazy. Thinking about it, that was right after I mentioned Carson."

"Interesting. But we need more evidence, because right now everything we have is all circumstantial. But why," he asked, sounding exasperated, "were you in here in the first place when you were supposed to be waiting for me?"

"I intended to, Cooper, honestly. But I heard him fire his gun." She motioned to the dead raccoon, still lying under the window. "He was just shooting that poor little critter, but I had no way of knowing that there wasn't a murder being committed, so I entered."

"I would have done the same," Cooper acknowledged. He shook his head at the body of the raccoon. "Talk about overkill. He shot it at point-blank range."

"He enjoys it," Sadie said. "Killing. You saw him at the hunt. And believe me, he's quite capable of treating women the same way that he does animals." She repeated some of Garcia's comments to him and the sheriff's mouth set in a grim line.

"So, what do you think the murders were about, if we go with the theory that it was him all along? Some kind of fetish for watching women being torn apart by wild animals?"

"I would say that suits what I've seen of him perfectly," Sadie said. "But what about Carson? We only have two bodies with conclusive tox reports of ketamine, and one of them is his, yet he doesn't fit the profile. Where does Carson come into this?"

"You tell me," Cooper said, shaking his head. "Figuring out psychopaths is your job. I just uphold the law."

He looked at her neck again. "How are you, Price, really? You've had a rough few days."

"Strangely enough," she replied, "I'm okay right now. I was more shook up by the bear attack than by the fight with Garcia. Perhaps because I got the better of Garcia." She grinned. "That's gonna dent his macho pride for a very long time, I reckon."

"I guess you're right." Cooper grinned back. Sadie felt relieved that some of their usual camaraderie had been restored, instead of the prickliness that he had been displaying since Rick showed up.

They started searching the cabin. Cooper stayed in the main room and kitchen while Sadie took the bedroom and tiny bathroom. Garcia didn't sleep on the floor but in a standard double bed, although his covering did look to be real fur.

More interesting than his bed sheets, though, was the glass display case that took up the length of one wall. She leaned down to look at the items in it, hardly able to take in what she was seeing.

Garcia seemed to be obsessed with bear trophies. There was a belt buckle adorned with what could only be bear fangs, and a pair of slippers fashioned from what looked like genuine bear paws, among other equally grisly items.

"Cooper! Come and look at this," she called.

"Wait; I think I've found something too," he called back. When he entered the bedroom, he gave a nod.

"Ketamine," he announced. "A way bigger stash than I think you would need for one hunt. Didn't Garcia say he hadn't used this cabin for months before this?"

"Yes," Sadie murmured. "And look at these. Is it even legal, collecting trophies like this?"

"Bonsor would know more about that than me," Cooper said with only a hint of snark, "but in Alaska, trophy hunting is legal. Although changes in protections often occur with each change in president. There has been a relaxing of regulations. A lot of the locals were in an uproar about it." He frowned.

"What is it?"

"I can't remember exactly," Cooper said, "but there's a type of trophy hunting that's illegal still. Something to do with the practice of bear baiting, but I can't remember the details."

Sadie made a mental note to ask Rick about bear baiting and trophy hunters but decided it would be wiser not to mention that to the sheriff right now, not while the atmosphere between them was friendly again.

As though he had guessed her thoughts, Cooper gave an awkward cough.

"Let's get this stuff bagged up and processed," he said. "Once Garcia is stitched up, I'll get him in for interrogation. I'll need a statement from you about the attack, too."

"Sure," Sadie said. "Let me know if you need me, although I should probably keep away from the interrogation given the circumstances."

Cooper grinned again. "You're one helluva detective, Price," he said. "I'm starting to make a habit of apologizing for not listening to you."

"No apology needed," Sadie assured him. "This has been a crazy case so far."

Cooper nodded. "Sure has. And it isn't over yet," he said.

*

There was no change in her father's condition. She hadn't really expected there to be, yet nevertheless the disappointment was bitter in her chest when she walked into his room and sat down by his bedside. The familiar beeping of the various monitors remained, a steady constant at each visit, reminding her that her father was clinging to life.

He would be a stubborn bastard to the end, no doubt, she thought wryly.

She wondered what he would have thought of this case. She suspected that Garcia would have been a man that her father admired up until his arrest. A man's man, a hunter. Keeping to the old Alaskan traditions, with no time for "all this silly environmentalism" as her father had always called it. Never mind that recent polls revealed that most Alaskans did want regulations on hunting, and care taken to preserve the beautiful wild lands of the most northern US state.

Still, she suspected that he would have been proud of the way that she had seen off Garcia. Violence and brute strength were the only languages that her father knew.

Or at least, they had been. Lying here, wasting away from cancer as much as the recent cardiac arrest, he had no fight left in him. He was hanging on to the last tendrils out of life out of sheer belligerence.

She sat back in the hard chair by the side of the bed, wondering why hospital furniture was always so uncomfortable. Probably to deter visitors from staying too long and getting in the way of the doctors and nurses. It certainly wasn't doing much for her bruised and aching body.

Garcia had taken her by surprise, and she couldn't help thinking that had she been just a little slower or more hesitant, their encounter could have ended very differently. He had no qualms about hurting her. But then, if he was indeed their killer, why would he?

He had to be, she realized. Even if his motive seemed weak— staging the attacks to initiate a hunt so he could bring a mankiller or two down—it would make sense to him. A decade with the FBI had taught her that people could kill for surprisingly little, when it came down to it.

But they still needed something more concrete if he was to be convicted. A hotshot lawyer could pull apart the evidence they currently had. Of course, it wasn't her job to prosecute and sentence— once it went to trial it was out of her hands, other than being called as a witness—but something about it was niggling at her.

Their best hope was that Garcia confessed in the chance of getting a more lenient sentence. But she didn't think he would; Garcia seemed too proud for that.

She looked over at her father then, wondering if he, too, would ever confess. Finally tell her what he knew about Jessica's disappearance and death. It was looking likely that he was never going to get the chance, and the unfairness of it made Sadie want to scream at the world. Why was her sister's case the only one she couldn't seem to crack?

The nurse came in, looking sympathetically at her. Earlier, she had brought Sadie a hot drink, but now her hands were empty.

"Ms. Price?" she said gently. "It's getting late. Why don't you go home and get some sleep? You look very tired."

"Thanks," Sadie mumbled. She knew she looked like shit. She couldn't remember the last time she had even had her hair done or bought something new.

"We will call you if there is any change," the nurse assured her, as she always did when Sadie left.

She was making her way out of the hospital when Rick called.

"Sadie!" he gasped. "I've just heard about Garcia attacking you. I'm so sorry. I had no idea that he would go that far."

"Don't worry, he came out of it worse than I did," Sadie reassured him.

Rick's voice dropped. "Is it true you've arrested him for staging the bear attacks?"

"Yes," Sadie confirmed, not surprised that he knew already. News traveled fast around Anchorage, even out in the hinterlands. Gossip was as good as currency here and given that the hunt had been the talk of the area over the last two days, this new development would be nothing short of sensational.

"My God," Rick said, sounding stunned. "I thought he was up to something but…" His voice trailed off. Sadie didn't blame him for being shocked. She dealt with killers on a regular basis and yet this case had confounded her. Rick was a zoologist. She suspected animal behavior was a lot simpler to decipher.

"The sheriff will probably want to talk to you about Garcia," she told Rick. "We are still trying to figure out the hows and whys. Do you know anything about bear baiting?"

There was a pause. "A little. It's not my favorite subject. Listen, why don't you come over? I'll make you a coffee and you can ask me all the questions you want. I'll help if I can, although I'm still shocked by all this to be honest. Are you sure you're okay?"

"I'm fine," she said again, wondering how true that was as she thought about Rick's offer. She was exhausted, yet at the same time the adrenaline was surging around her body, and she wasn't sure she was ready to go back to the saloon yet. Especially when she was likely to be peppered with questions about Garcia. A coffee with Rick sounded tempting.

"Sure," she said, and she could almost hear him smile on the other end. "I'm on my way right now."

Perhaps she could find out something useful on Garcia.

CHAPTER TWENTY THREE

Sheriff Cooper walked into the hospital room where Garcia was lying in a bed, one arm cuffed to the rail. He had a bandage around his head and stitches in his face, but he looked far from subdued, scowling as he saw the sheriff approach.

The state trooper guarding his room looked relieved to see the sheriff and Cooper felt bad that he was about to let him down.

"I'm not here to take over. I just wanted a quick word with our patient here. Any word on when we can take him down to the station for questioning?"

"The doctor wants to keep him here overnight," the trooper told him. "He's got a concussion."

"Good," Cooper said, loud enough for Garcia to hear. "Perhaps he will think twice before he throws his weight around again with a trained federal agent."

He sat down by Garcia's bed, grinning at the handcuffed man. "Looks like you picked on the wrong person, Billy."

Garcia just glared at him, and Cooper saw the sheer violence in his eyes. He knew a dangerous man when he saw one, and he wondered why he hadn't suspected the man before. But until the traces of ketamine had been found in Carson's body, there had been no real evidence to support Agent Price's theory.

Cooper really had to stop doubting her. This wasn't the first time he had dismissed her hunches, only for them to turn out to be right on the nose.

"You got something you wanna say, Cooper?" Garcia snarled. "Because this doesn't look like an interrogation room to me."

"Well, if you want to confess I can take your statement here," Cooper offered. Garcia snorted in derision.

"I've got nothing to confess. Whatever you and that bitch are trying to blame on me, I didn't do it."

Cooper bristled at Garcia's tone and saw a slow, mocking smile spread across the other man's face. "You like her, don't you, Sheriff? Shame that Bonsor seems to have gotten there before you. You should have taken your chances when you had them. She's a hot little piece. Or did she not fancy you?"

"Shut your mouth," Cooper snarled, a hot wave of anger running up his spine even as he told himself to stay cool and not let a suspect rile him. He had dealt with cleverer men than Billy Garcia, but it seemed that Sadie Price was his weak point.

Garcia laughed, showing even, white teeth with large, sharp canines, like a wolf. "You sure jump to her defense quick don't you, Sheriff? Got a little crush there? Must be a blow to lose out to a pussy like Bonsor, crying over a goddamn bear. I bet Price will eat him for breakfast. She needs a real man, and if you hadn't interrupted us, she might have just got one."

Cooper swallowed his rage, remembering why he was here. Deliberately relaxing his body, he sat back in the chair and looked pointedly at the handcuffs on Garcia's wrist.

"You might want to rethink your attitude, Garcia. Right now, I'm your best friend. And the more you can tell me, the easier a judge will go on you. You might want to stop talking that way about Agent Price, because if I record those comments, it isn't going to look too good for you in court. Considering that you have also been charged for assaulting her."

Garcia went red. "She assaulted me!"

"She defended herself against you," Cooper corrected calmly, back in the driver's seat again. "Because you were trying to 'give her a real man,' remember? It didn't look like that was going so well for you when I turned up, Billy. It seems she outmanned you. It must be a blow to that ego of yours, getting beaten up by a woman."

The veins in Garcia's neck bulged and for a moment Cooper thought he was going to try and snap the cuffs. Garcia's jaw worked furiously, and Cooper smiled again. "Feeling frustrated there, Billy? It will be even worse when you're locked up in jail. And no matter how much of an alpha male you think you are, you will be crying like Bonsor after a few weeks in maximum security."

Some of the tension went out of Garcia and his shoulders slumped, although his eyes burned with hatred for the sheriff.

"I haven't done anything wrong," Garcia insisted. "Your little Fed bitch attacked me, and I had nothing to do with the bear attacks. They're just bear attacks. You're both crazy."

"Unfortunately for you," Cooper told him, casually draping one foot over the other knee and inspecting his nails, "we have evidence that says otherwise. And points to you. You won't be walking out of here alone, Billy. You'll be coming straight down to the station with me for interrogation and then you'll be in county jail. I wonder what bail the judge will post. Serial killers are none too popular around here. Like I said, a confession would be in your best interests. Convince a judge to go a little easier on you."

Garcia shook his head, his eyes widening as he showed fear for the first time. "You're trying to frame me," he accused. "Setting me up. Whatever's going on it ain't got nothin' to do with me. I just wanted to kill some bears."

He seemed genuine, Cooper thought, having a flickering moment of doubt. Then he remembered the trophies in Garcia's room. And the accusations against him that he had read in the file that Sadie had obtained from the FBI field office.

"You sure about that?"

"I'm not a violent man," Garcia insisted. Cooper knew that was a lie.

"That's not what your ex-wife says, is it, Billy?"

Garcia's dark eyes narrowed. "How do you know about her? All charges were dropped, because she's a lying bitch."

The sheriff shrugged. "It happens, I guess. But she hasn't been the only woman to claim you assaulted her and then drop the charges, has she? The Feds have a nice file on you, Garcia. Seems you've been a suspect in a few high-profile illegal trophy-hunting cases, but you've always evaded charges. You're a liability, Billy. Game and Wildlife moved you out here to the outskirts of Anchorage to get you out of the way, didn't they? Because you were becoming an embarrassment."

Garcia's eyes were bulging again, but there was no real fight left in him, Cooper could sense it. He pressed his point further.

"You won't have a job now, not after attempting to assault a federal agent. You'll be disgraced, Billy. That's before we get into the staged bear attacks. That's murder. Planned and premeditated. You're lucky we don't have the death penalty. You're in enough trouble," Cooper finished, softening his tone in faux sympathy, "a confession really would be the best thing you could do for yourself right now."

Garcia just glared at him as Cooper stood up out of his chair and made to leave. "I'll leave you to think about it, Billy. I'll see you down at the station in the morning. You might want to call your lawyer."

"I won't have anything to say about no murders then either," Garcia insisted. "And my lawyer will be suing your ass."

"If you say so, Billy," Cooper said cheerfully, walking out of the room.

"I'll get someone to relieve you for the night shift," he promised the trooper at the door before he walked down the corridor. He thought about looking in on Agent Price, who had said she was going to visit her father, but decided to leave her to it. She wouldn't welcome him intruding on a vulnerable moment. She wasn't the sort of woman who appreciated being thought of as vulnerable either. If she had heard the comments Garcia had just made about her, she would have busted his face up all over again.

Cooper scowled to himself as he thought about the way Garcia had spoken about her and Bonsor. It had riled him, and it riled him even more that Garcia had picked up on it. *You like her, don't you, Sheriff?*

Cooper decided not to pursue that particular train of thought, thinking instead about Garcia's insistence that he was innocent. He didn't believe him, of course. He had made enough mistakes on this case as it was, and now that they had a viable suspect firmly in custody and actual tangible evidence, he couldn't start having doubts again now.

There could be no doubt that the attacks were staged. Someone had lured those bears to the victims, who had been sedated on ketamine. It all made sense now. Why there had been no screams heard by anyone in the vicinity, no evidence of any attempt to fight the bears off. All the victims had guns. The bear attacks were cold-blooded murders, just as Price had said all along.

But what if Garcia wasn't the killer? Cooper felt unsettled as he considered the possibility that the man wasn't lying about his innocence. There was no concrete evidence, after all, and only a weak motive.

Cooper pushed the doubts away as he walked outside and got into the snowcat, looking forward to an early night before he started to formally interrogate the man with the deputy the next day. He would miss having Price by his side. They complemented each other well in the interview room. Whatever Garcia was hiding, they could get it out of him.

Garcia *had* to be the killer, the sheriff told himself firmly as he drove off.

Because if he wasn't, then there was still a murderer out there.

CHAPTER TWENTY FOUR

Sadie sat at the kitchen table, watching Rick make coffee. Rick was staying in a cozy cabin nearer to town that couldn't be more different from Garcia's. No bear trophies or mounted heads on walls. Of course, it was only a temporary home, but she would have expected at least a few indications of the person currently residing there. Although the cabin was homely, it was also impersonal, as though anybody could live there. She wondered what his personal place was like, if he lived alone, or shared with others, and it struck her that she really knew very little about him.

Rick brought two large mugs of coffee to the table and sat opposite her. He smiled and lines crinkled around his eyes. He looked tired.

"I can't believe that idiot actually attacked you," he said, sounding angry. "I feel responsible."

"Responsible?" Sadie echoed, surprised. "Why would you be responsible for that?"

Rick sighed wearily, running a hand through his long hair. It looked dull, as though it needed washing, and he seemed stressed. It was a side of him she hadn't yet seen, but then the last few days had been enough to upset anyone's equilibrium.

"I put you onto Garcia by telling you all that stuff about him." Rick frowned. "I had no idea that any of this would happen. You being attacked, that poor cub being shot…"

"None of this is your fault," Sadie said emphatically. "If you hadn't told me, we would have caught up with him anyway. There was evidence on the bodies that would have led me to him. And the more we know about him, the more solid a case that we can build. As for the bear…that was Garcia's fault alone. You have been doing your best to protect them since all this started."

"Thank you," he said, gazing into her eyes. Sadie realized that she didn't feel the same magnetic pull to him, and it wasn't because he didn't look as handsome as usual. Perhaps she was just tired too.

He seemed to notice her lack of reaction and pulled back in his seat slightly. An almost annoyed look crossed his face and Sadie took a swig of her coffee to hide her sudden discomfort. She wasn't here to flirt.

"Well, I'm glad you're okay," he said amiably. Perhaps she had been imagining things. "What was it you wanted to know? I'm obviously happy to tell you anything that could help. I can't quite believe he has been a killer in our midst all this time. Do you think there could be other murders we don't know about?"

"It wouldn't surprise me," Sadie said, "but there haven't been many humans killed by bears, so unless he's changed his MO it's unlikely. He could have been building up to it, though. Serial killers—because that's what this is now—rarely spring out of nowhere. Which is what I wanted to ask you about—you said that you thought Garcia was a sadist. Do you know anything about bear baiting? Like, with trophy hunters?"

Rick was listening intently as she spoke and when she mentioned bear baiting, he winced.

"It's a nasty practice," he said, "and has been outlawed for some time now, although trophy hunting groups keep trying to overturn the ruling. Hunters looking for trophies will leave piles of food lying around to attract bears, then shoot them while they are distracted by it. As well as being unsustainable and damaging bear populations, it's dangerous. The food used is human food, and so it habituates bears into coming into closer contact with humans and associating human areas with feeding grounds. It's the exact opposite of everything the Game and Wildlife Division stands for. But I've heard rumors."

"About Garcia?"

"Yes," Rick confirmed. "But I have no concrete evidence. I can talk to others who might know more, though. Garcia is popular with hunters and trappers, but all of our conservation agents hate him."

Sadie nodded, thinking hard. If Garcia didn't confess, they had little concrete evidence that would tie him to the attack scenes. Witnesses who could testify to his character might be useful.

"It would make sense," she said slowly as another thought occurred to her. "That's how he encouraged the mama bear to attack, isn't it? By using baiting methods."

Rick nodded solemnly. "I know Garcia has spent a lot of time around here the past few winters. He could have been working on the whole group of them. You will be lucky if there are no more attacks. I would definitely recommend that no more humans move into the area."

Sadie thought about Clarity's planned resort. Would McAllister still go ahead after all this?

"The trouble is," Rick went on, "that too much land is being bought up, and the bears are being pushed further and further back. That means when wild food is scarce, they have no options but to come on to human settlements. Then we go all crazy and want to kill the bears, when it is us who are destroying their habitats in the first place." He looked angry again, his eyes hard. Sadie thought about how she had initially found his passion attractive, but right now it almost seemed to border on fanaticism.

It wasn't that he was wrong—she agreed with him, in fact—but the look in his eyes in that moment reminded her of Anchorage's local fundamentalist preacher, who could often be found around town railing against the heathens.

"How did you get into all this?" she asked, genuinely interested. "Did you always know what you wanted to do? I knew I would join the FBI at fifteen." *After my sister was murdered,* she finished silently.

"I've always loved animals and conservation, yes," he told her. "Especially bears. I didn't know exactly what route to go down at first, though. I got a degree in zoology and biology in college and then ending up working for a private land grant caretaker."

"What happened there?" Sadie asked when Rick went quiet.

"It was sold and developed into a residential area. I saw the deforestation and animal displacement and the damage and death it caused—it disgusted me. Then I came to Game and Wildlife. My dream, though, is to create a safe haven for bears. A wildlife park where hunting and trapping are forbidden."

"That sounds lovely." Sadie took a last swig of her coffee.

"Do you want a refill?"

"Sure. Sugar and caffeine are exactly what I need right now," she said with a laugh as Rick stood up and took her mug. He stood with his back to her as he took coffee and sugar out of the cupboard and filled the coffeemaker but continued to talk to her.

"Honestly, what we are doing to the land as a species is disgusting. Human encroachment is like a virus. I despair of how we are ever going to stop it." His voice was hard again, his shoulders tense as he spoke.

"Mm-hmm," Sadie said, thinking again about the fanatical preacher. Calling humanity a virus seemed a bit strong.

"It may take desperate measures," he said. "I mean, it's about to happen here, isn't it? Thanks to McAllister and his insatiable greed."

Sadie froze. How did he now about that? She had never mentioned it to him, and as far as she knew it wasn't yet common knowledge. It couldn't be, not until the final plans were through. Perhaps the locals whose cabins were being targeted had complained to Game and Wildlife, she thought.

But she couldn't shake the sudden wave of suspicion that swept over her, even though she told herself not to be silly. They had their guy. Garcia had the motive, means, and opportunity. And he was cruel to both animals and women. Rick loved bears with a passion. He wouldn't do anything that would get one of them killed.

Would he? She thought of the despair in his eyes and his blaming himself for the death of the cub, and suddenly she wasn't so sure. Sacrificing one to save the many was a common theme of fanatics.

Rick had gone quiet and was rummaging around in the cupboard.

"Have you run out?" she asked. "I should probably get going anyway. But thank you for the information about bear baiting, that could be really important."

"Oh, no, I was just looking for my sweeteners. I've made your coffee, look." He poured it out and brought it over. Sadie decided she would drink it quickly and then get home where she could think clearly. Look at that file on Garcia—and maybe see if there was anything in Rick's past, too.

Rick stood slightly behind her as he read out to place the mug on the table, and a few scalding drops fell on her neck.

"Ow," Sadie exclaimed, startled. She turned to take the cup from him and then felt another sensation, this time just under her hairline where her hair was swept up into a bun in an attempt to tame her curls. A sharp, hot sensation like a snake bite.

Or a needle.

Sadie jumped up, spinning around and lunging out of the way even as she knew it was too late. She could feel whatever he had injected her with filling her veins. She tried to steady herself and reach for her gun, but her limbs felt somehow heavy and soft, and she couldn't coordinate her movements. Her vision started to blur as she stared at Rick in shock and horror.

He watched her calmly, a regretful little smile on his face. "I'm sorry, Sadie," he said casually, as though he was just apologizing for the spilled coffee.

Sadie opened her mouth to protest but no words came out. The room started to spin around her, and she felt herself sinking to the floor, her hand still fumbling helplessly at her side for her gun.

"Don't worry, Sadie," she heard him say, somewhere far above her. "It will be quick."

Then she blacked out.

CHAPTER TWENTY FIVE

Fog. The awareness that she was moving or being moved, and a vague feeling that she needed to wake up; that there was something that she needed to do, but her body and brain wouldn't cooperate. Her limbs were heavy, as though weighted down, and she felt as though she was drunk. When she tried to open her eyes, her surroundings whirled around her like a moving kaleidoscope. A wave of nausea hit her, and she closed her eyes again, trying to work out where she was.

She heard voices, muffled as though speaking through water, and tried to focus on them, because she had a sense that something important was being said.

Not voices. One voice. Rick.

Why was she with Rick?

Snatched, fragmented memories came back to her, too disordered for her to piece them together. The bear hunt, with the mama bear charging through the water at Garcia, its teeth bared to kill. Sheriff Cooper looking at the scratches on her neck, radiating with disapproval. Her father, lying in hospital surrounded by tubes and beeping machines. Jessica. Always Jessica.

Jessica was trying to tell her something.

Wake up, Sadie. Wake up.

Although her body couldn't move, it felt like an immense physical effort to try and focus her consciousness into the present. To focus on the drone of Rick's voice through the creeping fog in her mind.

She tried to open her eyes again. The world lurched and span, and she shut them again quickly. Okay, that wasn't going to work. She focused on her body, on her limbs that felt like cement and yet also somehow as though they belonged to someone else.

She was sitting. Yet moving. How did that work? If only she could see.

Wake up, Sadie.

The hum of the engine became apparent through the fog as a little more consciousness returned. Rick's voice became louder.

Rick. She must be in his car. As the realization became clear, the moments before her blackout exploded back into her memory.

She had been in his kitchen. Talking about the case. About Garcia, the murderer.

Except he wasn't.

It was Rick. Rick had drugged her with ketamine just like he had done to Bobby Carson, Jane Winters, and possibly Marie DuVale too.

He was going to kill her.

She wanted to—needed to—scream, but her body wouldn't obey her commands. Instead, she concentrated again on his voice, trying to make out what he was saying.

His voice was almost sing-song, as though he was telling her a pleasant story. She had to use all the concentration that she could muster to understand what was being said to her.

"If only you hadn't gotten involved, Sadie," he said, his tone remorseful. "You were too thorough. Treating the attacks like crime scenes when anyone else—even that sheriff of yours—would have taken it at face value. But you couldn't just leave it, could you? I suppose that's what makes you a good detective. It's a pity because I never wanted to hurt you. I liked you." He sounded almost accusatory, as though Sadie was at fault.

"As soon as I saw you, I knew you could be trouble," he went on. "You asked too many questions, and had no right even being there. But I didn't realize at first that you were actively investigating. I thought I was in the clear. It should have been easy. But you kept going on about the food at Winters's cabin, about a trail. So I tried to throw you off. Make sure that the scene at Carson's cabin was as natural as possible.

"It nearly worked too, didn't it? But I saw your face when the sheriff shut your line of inquiry down and I knew I would have to do more to throw you off the scent. I knew you wouldn't just give up. And you would have ruined everything. So I started dropping hints about Garcia. You picked up on them right away." He laughed, chuckling to himself as he drove. "Ms. Hotshot FBI Agent, derailed by a pretty face."

Sadie felt a wash of shame. He was right; she hadn't suspected him, and she should have. She should have suspected everyone.

But it wasn't just because Rick was handsome. She knew better than that. She realized with a stab of terror that the man next to her was a complete sociopath. Charming, manipulative…and thoroughly dangerous. As much as she might have wanted to believe that she was immune, the hallmark of a sociopath was their ability to fool even the most dedicated professional.

Even so, this hadn't happened to her before. She had dropped her guard, and this was where it had gotten her. She had missed the signs; they all had.

Blackness washed over her, bringing a wave of despair with her. She could feel the fog threatening to drag her down again, to take her under. But she knew that if she succumbed to it, it could be the last thing she ever did. She needed to think. To form some kind of plan to rescue herself.

But how was she supposed to do that when she couldn't move or speak?

Rick was talking to her again. Or in reality, to himself, because he had no way of knowing that she was able to hear him.

"It was a stroke of luck, Garcia turning up," he told her conversationally, "even though I was angry at first. I knew the bastard would want as many kills to his name as possible. My first thought was for the bears...especially the cubs. I knew he would want them as trophies. You've seen his cabin. He's evil."

Rick took a deep breath, sounding almost choked up. "He deserves to go to jail," he continued. "He's a predator...no, not even that. A scavenger. Taking trophies from beautiful animals who have more right to life than he ever will. But framing him was easy once I got the idea. We work at the same place after all. It was easy enough for me to borrow one of the standard Jeeps and get my hands on a stash of ketamine. I knew Garcia wouldn't miss it; he's got enough of his own. And of course, motive is easy...everyone knows he's a sadist."

There was no sense of irony in Rick's words, Sadie realized. He really believed that he was the good guy, and the total opposite of Garcia.

There were few things more dangerous than an idealistic sociopath with a cause.

"You must be wondering why I've done this," Rick said as though they were actually engaged in a dialogue. "And I can assure you, Sadie, it wasn't easy. But what choice did I have? I had to do something to stop the constant developments and the encroachment onto natural habitats. Grizzlies aren't a protected species, yet their numbers are dwindling, thanks to people like Garcia and the land developers. Black bears are going extinct, did you know that? The grizzlies will be next. Bears are the lynchpin of the local eco system. The top of the chain. If they can be wiped off the map, what's to stop us destroying the rest of the wildlife? It can't be allowed to happen. I had to do something," he repeated. Sadie wondered if he was trying to convince himself.

"I heard about the Clarity plans from a girl I was dating who works there. Don't worry," he assured her, "you don't need to be jealous. It was a means to an end, that's all. Once I knew what was being planned, I knew the only way to stop it would be something big. Something that would not just scare people away from that spot but also make them think twice about continually encroaching on the bears' habitat. This was the best way.

"Of course," he continued sadly, "it meant making a sacrifice. One of the bears would have to turn killer. I had my eye on the big male at first, but it turned out that he was too skittish around humans. The mother bear was the obvious choice because they are always more aggressive. She made a noble sacrifice."

As though she had a choice. As though the animal had gone willingly along with Rick's plan rather than being slaughtered needlessly, for feeding habits that he had instilled in her. Sadie felt sick, and it wasn't just from the ketamine.

"The young one wasn't supposed to die," Rick hissed. "That was Garcia. I hoped I could protect them from him. But he will get his just deserts now. Even if he isn't found guilty, he will never work for Game and Wildlife again. Maybe one day I will get my chance to feed him to the bears," he snarled, sounding wholly unlike himself. Or at least, unlike the Rick that Sadie had thought she had been getting to know. That Rick was just a mask, cleverly designed to throw her off the scent. Who would expect the sensitive, animal-loving zoologist to have a hand in this?

Sadie was fighting with herself to attempt to move, but her body still just wouldn't obey, as though it was a completely separate object from her mind. But her mind was gradually becoming clearer and sharper. She slightly opened one eye to find that her vision was still blurry, but the world seemed to be the right side up again.

She could see pine branches outside the window, and then a clearing with a cabin. They were in the pine woods near the mountains.

Where the bear attacks had happened—or rather, been orchestrated.

Sadie tried not to panic as it sank in just what Rick was planning to do.

She was going to be the next victim.

But the mama bear was dead. Was he really going to sacrifice another of his beloved animals for what he believed was the greater good?

Rick Bonsor was certifiably insane. Never in her decade as a criminal behavior expert had she come across anything like this. No wonder he had been able to fool her.

Now she had to figure out how the hell she was going to escape when her body was completely incapacitated.

"We're here," Rick said cheerfully as he brought his Bronco to a halt. "At least you won't be alone, Sadie. I'm glad about that."

He got out and she could hear his footsteps walking away. Then a cabin door opening and an unfamiliar voice.

At least you won't be alone...

He was going to kill someone else. Sadie peeped from under her eyelashes, not wanting Rick to catch her and realize that she was conscious. Through the blurry images she could just make out his shape, and that of a woman with white hair. An older woman? She tried to think about who she knew that lived alone up here. Then it dawned on her, and she screamed silently inside her head.

Mrs. Benton had lived up this way even when Sadie was a kid. She and Jessica used to visit her for fresh cookies and hot cocoa when they were playing in the woods. There hadn't been so many bears around then, not that their father took much notice of where they were or what they were doing in any case. He was too busy in the saloon, drowning his grief.

Rick was coming back. Sadie shut her eyes again, still silently screaming in frustration. If only she could get some movement back, she could take Rick out. Unlike Garcia, she suspected that he was no fighter. Even unarmed she had a good chance of taking him down...but not if she couldn't move.

As Rick lifted her out of the truck and carried her over to the cabin there was nothing Sadie could do. She had no choice but to lie helplessly in his arms.

"Oh, that's little Sadie Price!" she heard Mrs. Benton exclaim. "What happened? I don't remember her ever having seizures as a kid."

"She had a traumatic head injury down in D.C.," Rick lied smoothly to the old woman. "I think that's bringing them on. This is the worst one I've seen; I just can't bring her around. And the way the roads are right now I'm afraid I won't get her to Anchorage in time."

He carried her into the cabin. She felt the warmth from Mrs. Benton's old wood stove and was aware of softness around her as she was laid on cushions. Sensations were returning...but she still couldn't move. When Pete had explained the effects of ketamine to her, he had said this state could last for hours.

Which meant she would be fully awake but unable to move as the bear devoured her.

"Well, she's breathing fine." She felt a cool hand on her forehead. "I'll call for the medic helicopter. Hopefully, there's no brain damage."

That made Sadie think of her father. She would never see him again. And for once, that grieved her.

She would never see Caz again either, or little Jenny, or Deputy Jane Cooper. Her friends.

She would never see the sheriff again. For some reason, that bothered her most of all.

Mrs. Benton had walked away, no doubt to call emergency services. Sadie risked opening an eye and saw the shadowy figure of Rick coming up behind her. She tried to make her mouth work, to make some kind of noise to alert the old woman to the evil that had invaded her home, but the most she could manage was a tiny, almost inaudible croak.

They didn't hear her. She saw the shape of Mrs. Benton fall to the ground, and Rick turn around and come toward her on the couch.

The room tipped over.

Then Sadie blacked out again.

CHAPTER TWENTY SIX

When she came around, it was dark. Or she just couldn't see.

This time she felt completely disembodied, as though she had no body at all. But she could see better, she realized as she watched Rick moving around through the gloom. He had turned off the lights inside the cabin.

Where was Mrs. Benton? Sadie couldn't turn her head, but she swiveled her eyes and could make out the woman's body lying on the floor next to the couch, just in the corner of her vision. She had no way of knowing if she was dead or alive, unconscious or, like her, trapped in a disembodied limbo.

She closed her eyes again as Rick came closer, not wanting him to see that she was awake and knock her out again. Then she would have no chance of regaining any movement before the bear turned up. But closing her eyes meant that she couldn't see what the zoologist was doing.

Luckily, Rick decided to continue with the monologue that he had started in the truck.

She soon realized that she would rather he stopped talking, because lying here helpless, his words were terrifying.

"I'll need to be careful not to leave an obvious trail this time, won't I, Sadie? Now that you've alerted the sheriff to that particular detail. Instead, Mrs. Benton has just left her rubbish out on the porch. People get forgetful as they get older. And then a raccoon got to it." He tutted, sounding sad.

Sadie thought she had never hated anyone quite so much.

"Of course," he continued as he moved around the cabin, "I don't want to jeopardize the bear population. The mother bear's remaining cub already has a taste for human flesh, so he is the obvious culprit. And he's big enough to do plenty of damage. What a piece of luck that this woman knows you. Now there's no need to worry about a reason for you being here.

"I will do my best to protect the young bear. But either way this will save the rest of them. A whole family of man-killing grizzlies in the area? There won't be any developments here now. People will think twice about living in bear country. I heard there have already been lots of these cabins vacated. It's working." He sounded unbearably smug. "Soon they will have their land back. Their rightful habitat. Without the fear of being hunted and baited."

He moved into the other room, still talking to himself, although Sadie could no longer make out what he was saying. Not that she wanted to. She had heard enough. His plan was ridiculous, but he might just get away with it. It made sense that the remaining cub would still seek out humans for food, especially now that his sibling and mother were gone. But Sadie's presence wouldn't be as easy to explain as he seemed to think. She wasn't the visiting type. Rick might not know that, but others would.

The sheriff would know that something was wrong with this whole set-up, she was sure of it. And he wouldn't let it slide. With all of the other suspects accounted for, surely now he would consider Rick as the culprit. They were running out of other options.

Unlike you, she reprimanded herself, wishing she could turn back the clock. She vowed to herself that if by some miracle she managed to get out of this, she would never fall for any man's charms again.

She could smell food. Salmon, in fact, coming toward her nose. Her stomach roiled as she felt Rick leaning over her and understood what he was doing.

He was baiting her. Making sure the hungry bear came straight to her. The salmon would just be the starter.

And she couldn't even fight back.

Feeling powerless, helpless, had always been Sadie's worst nightmare. She could face down the craziest villain and most sick psychopath as long as she could *do* something. Could fight. Rick had done the worst thing to her that anyone could possibly do.

She wanted to kill him.

He stepped back, standing over her for a long moment, and even though she knew it was futile Sadie prayed that he would have some kind of attack of conscience and change his mind.

Then he leaned down and brushed a tendril of hair from her cheek, before kissing her lightly on the lips like some twisted version of Sleeping Beauty.

"I won't forget you, Sadie. There could have really been something between us, if only you hadn't decided to stick your nose where it wasn't wanted."

His footsteps moved away, and she heard the door opening. He was leaving.

Which meant the bear would be coming soon. Rick must have located it already and would know how to lead it here. She was a sitting duck.

Then she realized that in her anger she was clenching her fists.

Her hands could move.

She held her breath, waiting for Rick to leave so she could test her limbs, wondering how much time she had before the grizzly arrived.

She heard him pause at the door.

"Bye then, Sadie," he said sadly. "I'll be back in the morning…to clean up. Then I'll call in the horrific attack I found on my morning rounds. I'm sure you'll be missed."

She heard the door shut behind him and his footsteps moving away from the cabin. Not until she heard the engine of his Bronco fading into the distance did she open her eyes.

The smell of salmon was everywhere. She looked over at Mrs. Benton—and realized that she could turn her head.

Feeling a rush of adrenaline, Sadie tried to sit up, but quickly realized she was nowhere near that mobile yet. She managed to lift her neck a few centimeters from the couch, only for her to lose her control and have her head thud back against the couch. She was hours away from being able to move properly.

But she could move her hands.

She wiggled them around, brushing them against her belt, and then smiled to herself as she realized the fatal, almost juvenile mistake that Rick had made.

He hadn't removed her holster. She was still armed.

Sadie fumbled for her gun, but her fingers felt thick and swollen and her wrists as though they were disconnected from her arm. The more she mentally pushed herself, the more her vision began to blur again.

Take it easy, she told herself. *Bit by bit.*

But she might not have time for that.

The minutes ticked by as she concentrated on getting the feeling back in her hands and moving them toward her holster…and her gun. At the same time, feeling was coming back elsewhere. She could move her mouth and head, and ever so slightly shift her weight against the couch. It wasn't much, but it showed that the sedative was wearing off.

Then she heard a low, choked groan next to her. Mrs. Benton. Like Sadie had been, she must be incapacitated but at least semi-conscious and aware of her surroundings.

The thought of the old woman being eaten alive by the young bear was too much for Sadie. She had to get them out of here and take Rick Bonsor down before he murdered any more people on his quest to save the wilds. With a huge effort she managed to place her hand on her holster.

Then she heard footsteps outside the cabin.

They weren't human.

She heard them on the wooden decking of the porch, heavy and pounding, and knew that the bear was approaching, drawn by the food that Rick had left for him to find, using the same baiting techniques that he had used earlier. She doubted he was able to see either the hypocrisy or the irony. He was too far gone, a madman with a cause.

The killer approaching her now, though, was much simpler. This one just wanted to eat her.

The cabin shook as the bear pushed against the door and Sadie felt the panic rising inside her. She could see the wood starting to splinter, but even making what felt like a superhuman effort to focus her energy and will, she only just managed to get the flap of her holster open before she had to pause for breath, exhausted. Black dots swam in front of her eyes, and she knew that if she pushed herself too hard she would pass out again.

Leaving herself and Mrs. Benton at the mercy of the young grizzly.

There was a loud crash and the middle of the wooden door splintered fully. She could see the bear's paws and snout as it started to tear off pieces of wood, making a hole big enough for it to enter.

Mrs. Benton groaned again.

There was another crash, and the bear lumbered its way into the room. Youngster or not, it was still huge, shaping up to be a giant as its mother had been. It sniffed the air and roared, and Sadie saw the size of its teeth and power of its jaws and shuddered. She carefully started to push her still partly unresponsive fingers into her holster, concentrating hard to get the movement right while trying to conserve energy for what she needed to do.

The bear sat back on its haunches and began sniffing the floor, gobbling up the pieces of salmon Rick had strategically placed around the room. It lumbered over toward Mrs. Benton, sniffing at her shirt. The woman could only make a frightened half whimper, her eyes rolling back in her forehead. Mercifully, she seemed to have fully lost consciousness, and Sadie wondered if it was the ketamine or just sheer fright.

Sadie's fingers brushed the handle of her pistol and closed around it. Holding her breath, she tried to draw it out of the holster, but struggled to judge how tight her grip was. Fumbling, she managed to slide it out, only for her to lose any sense of her grip.

The gun went clattering to the floor at the side of the couch. The bear looked up warily, sniffing the air again, but then went back to sniffing at the old woman. Rick had tucked a fish fillet into her shirt pocket.

The bear tore at the shirt, wolfing the fillet down in one mouthful and scratching the old woman's chest in the process. A bead of blood rolled down her neck. The bear's nostrils flared as it scented blood. Sadie needed to move now.

She rolled her body to the edge of the couch, letting her arm fall to the floor, right next to her pistol. Thank God, the barrel was facing the bear. If she could just slide her finger into the trigger guard, she might just be able to get some rounds off—hopefully in the direction of the bear.

The problem was trying to make sure she didn't hit Mrs. Benton. She hesitated, assessing the risk. The bear snarled over Mrs. Benton and started to pull at her skirt, shaking the old woman like a rag doll.

Sade had no choice. If she didn't attempt to shoot, she would watch the old woman get mauled to death in front of her.

She pushed her finger into the trigger guard and squeezed with as much force as she could manage while trying to angle the barrel of the gun squarely at the bear's head.

Five shots sounded, one after the other, making Sadie's ears ring.

The bear backed up and reared up onto its back legs, roaring.

The shots had gone wide, thudding into the walls of the cabin, but just as Sadie's stomach began to sink in despair, the bear turned around and lumbered back out of the cabin, spooked by the sound of the shots, just as it had been at the river when its mother and sibling had been killed by that very same noise.

Sadie collapsed back onto the couch, her breathing ragged. The bear had gone.

But they weren't out of the woods yet. It could come back, or another grizzly could turn up. And Rick Bonsor would be back in the morning to finish off anything that was left of them. She had to get them out of here and alert the sheriff to Rick's guilt before the zoologist realized his would-be victims were missing and made a run for it.

If she didn't, he would come back and kill them both.

It was her last thought as she tried to sit up, only for exertion to overwhelm her and darkness to once more swim in front of her eyes as she passed out.

CHAPTER TWENTY SEVEN

Sheriff Cooper groaned when the sound of his phone ringing woke him from a fractured sleep. He had been dreaming about a bear chasing him and Agent Price, and it had been so vivid that he had been able to feel its hot breath on the back of his neck.

He fumbled for his phone, frowning when he saw the time and the name of the caller.

Caz from the saloon, at two in the morning? This couldn't be good. No doubt a fight had kicked off between drunken locals, still pumped up from the hunt earlier.

But why would she phone him and not the station? As sleep cleared from his mind he sat up, fully awake, and with a feeling of foreboding.

"Caz? What's wrong?"

"I'm sorry to call you this late, Logan," she said, using his first name as she always had. He had stopped bothering to correct her, even though she was the only person outside of his immediate family who really used it. "I think something has happened to Sadie. Unless you know where she is?"

Cooper felt his heart rate speed up. Something was wrong with Sadie. It hadn't been all that long since the attractive agent had nearly died in his arms, and he still felt protective of her—although he tried his best not to show it, knowing it would only infuriate her. Sadie was fiercely independent.

"The last time I saw her, she was at the hospital visiting her father. Perhaps something happened and she stayed there?"

"No, I've already tried the hospital. She left there late this evening. I've tried to call her, and it's turned off. If she had plans to stay out, Logan, she would have told me so I didn't leave the door open. And if she was coming back late, she would have told me so she didn't wake Jenny up knocking. She's considerate like that."

Cooper nodded to himself, knowing that Caz was right.

Unless Agent Price was highly distracted…. His gut churned as he considered the possibility that Sadie was spending the night with the zoologist, Rick Bonsor. It was none of his business, he told himself. Price was a grown woman, and she could spend her nights with whoever she damn well pleased.

So why did the thought of it make him want to punch Bonsor's handsome face in?

"She's been getting close to that Bonsor guy," he said, trying to sound as nonchalant as possible and knowing that he just sounded uptight. "Maybe she's with him and has lost track of time?"

He shut his eyes against the immediate mental images of Sadie alone and intimate with another guy. Of course, the problem with mental images was that you couldn't stop seeing them.

"No," Caz said firmly. "She definitely would have told me if they had a date. That's why I'm worried. This just isn't like her. And you know she can be headstrong. What if she's gone sniffing around the crime scenes and ran into a bear...or worse? If there's a murderer still out there?" The usually tough Caz sounded on the verge of hysterics and Cooper realized just how worried she was.

"She wouldn't do that at this time of night," he said in his most soothing voice, even though even as he said it, he knew that was probably false. Sadie was a brilliant agent, but part of that brilliance was the fact that she often did take risks. If something important had occurred to her in the middle of the night, it wouldn't be out of character for her to go investigating alone.

But that still didn't explain why she hadn't told Caz not to wait up. No, he concluded, the most likely scenario was that she was with Bonsor and had gotten .... carried away.

"We have the culprit in custody," he assured Caz. "I'm sure she's fine, and I can't log a missing person report for twenty-four hours."

"I know, that's why I called you direct," Caz said with a sigh. "You're probably right, but I've just got a bad feeling about this, and I can't shift it."

Cooper looked at his clock and shook his head. He wouldn't be getting back to sleep now.

"Give it a little longer and if she isn't back, I'll go out and have a look, okay?"

"Thank you, Logan," the bartender said, sounding grateful. Cooper ended the call and lay back down on his pillows, staring at the ceiling.

The minutes ticked by agonizingly slowly. Cursing, he picked his phone back up and called Sadie's number. As Caz had said, the line was dead. Swallowing his not inconsiderable pride, Cooper tried the number he had for Rick Bonsor, wondering what the hell he was supposed to say about why he was looking for Agent Price at this time of night. Sadie would expect that Caz would be worried about her, but he could just imagine the smirk on Bonsor's face as he informed the sheriff that she was with him.

But that was just the thing, he realized as he reviewed his own thoughts. Sadie *would* expect Caz to be worried about her. So, if she was just out with Bonsor or anywhere else, then why hadn't she called?

Bonsor's phone rang out. Cooper tried again, only to get the same response. Frustrated, he threw his cell phone down onto his bed and spent a few more minutes glaring at the ceiling.

There was no way he was going to get back to sleep. He got up and pulled on some pants and a T-shirt, then went over to the basin and slashed his face with icy water. The small electric light above the basin sputtered into life and he examined his reflection critically. The nighttime gloom deepened the circles under his eyes and the creases on his forehead. He was mid-thirties but lately, after a spate of stressful cases, he felt more like mid-fifties.

He had never been vain, but Cooper saw the way women looked at him. Even Caz became uncharacteristically coquettish when he was around. But he was no match for Bonsor, who looked more like a film star than a zoologist. No wonder Price liked him.

Cooper snapped off the light, telling himself to get a grip. He wasn't interested in Sadie Price.

Okay, so she was attractive. And smart. And funny. And a damn good detective.

She also infuriated the life out of him. It would never work. They would be terrible for each other.

So why did he still feel so damn jealous?

Moving quietly so as not to wake his sister, Cooper went quietly downstairs to make coffee. The Coopers lived in a large lodge, with spare rooms that they often rented out to boarders. Price had stayed once, when a snowstorm had prevented her making it back to Anchorage and the ramshackle motel that she had been staying in at the time.

He hadn't been able to sleep that night either, acutely aware of her sleeping just across the hall.

As he stirred sugar into a strong black coffee, he resigned himself to the fact that yes, he had some misplaced feelings for Agent Sadie Price. They had been thrown together on a tough case and worked closely together ever since. They had saved each other's lives. Of course he cared about her. Anything more than that, he had to let go of. She had made her choice.

How can she make a choice when you didn't let her know she had one? a treacherous voice whispered inside him. He shut it straight down. He wasn't getting into a rivalry with Bonsor over a woman. It wasn't his style.

But as he sat at the kitchen table in the dark, nursing a huge mug of coffee, Cooper started to think about the possibility of Price being with the zoologist in a different light.

Caz was right. Even if she was on a date with Bonsor—and it seemed the most likely place for her to be—she would have let the bartender know. Certainly, if she had decided to stay the night.

So, assuming that's where Sadie was, why hadn't she called? Cooper ran through the possibilities in his mind.

She hadn't realized the time... Perhaps, but sooner or later she would have, and then she would call.

She had gotten drunk and passed out... He couldn't imagine that at all.

Which seemed to leave only one explanation.

She was in some kind of danger.

With Bonsor? Cooper shook his head at his own thoughts. The zoologist might be smarmy and had, in the sheriff's opinion, moved in on Sadie far too quickly, but he didn't seem the violent type. But then hadn't Sadie told him stories about killers who fit that exact profile? The charming sociopath that you would never suspect.

The more he thought about it, the more it seemed a viable possibility that Bonsor wasn't all that he seemed. Realistically, though, how would he hurt Sadie Price? Just hours before, she had taken down Garcia, who had turned out to be not just a bloodthirsty hunter but a killer too.

Or was he? Remembering the way the man had protested his innocence, Cooper got up and started to pace the room as a different narrative started to take shape. What if Garcia really wasn't their guy? As Cooper had said himself, the evidence was largely circumstantial.

And he could think of only one other person who would have access to the bears, who knew his way around the creatures and would be able to get his hands on the ketamine used to subdue them.

Rick Bonsor.

The more he thought about it, the more obvious it seemed. The only thing he couldn't fathom was Bonsor's motive, but he could worry about that later. Right now, if his hunch was right, then Sadie was in serious trouble.

Cooper sprang into action, grabbing his sweater, jacket, badge, and gun. He wasn't sure where Bonsor was staying while he was in the hinterlands, but if he couldn't get his location from Game and Wildlife then he would go to the hospital and drag it out of Garcia. If Bonsor wasn't home, then he would start searching the pine woods.

As he left the lodge and jumped into the snowcat, Cooper prayed that he was wrong.

And that if he was right, he was able to get to Sadie in time before she became the killer's next victim.

CHAPTER TWENTY EIGHT

She could hear birds singing.

Sadie opened her eyes, relieved to see that the room was no longer spinning and her vision was clear. She sat up, her whole body aching, then realized that she could move. Her body felt thick and heavy, but she could move.

Maybe she could even stand.

She tried and promptly threw up all over the couch. Groaning, she crouched down instead as a wave of dizziness overcame her, closing her eyes as she waited for it to pass. When she opened her eyes again, she saw the gun lying near her feet and picked it up. She needed to reload. Fumbling with her holster, she inserted fresh ammo into her pistol with clumsy, shaky fingers. The bear hadn't come back, but sooner or later, Rick would.

And she would be ready for him.

Just as soon as she stopped feeling dizzy.

Her head was pounding, and her tongue felt swollen and fuzzy in her mouth. Why some people took ketamine as a "recreational" drug, Sadie couldn't fathom. She felt terrible.

Mrs. Benton was unconscious on the floor, her clothes torn. Sadie crawled over to her, checking the scratches on her chest from the bear, relieved to see that they were superficial, and the woman's breathing looked even.

She needed to get her an ambulance. Remembering there was a working phone as the older woman had been calling emergency services to help Sadie when they had arrived, Sadie stood up carefully and looked around the room. She also scanned the walls for a clock, wondering how long she had been out and what time it was. The birdsong indicated that it was morning, but it was still dark outside. That didn't mean much; at this time of year sunrise could be as late as ten in the morning.

Feeling disoriented, Sadie walked over to the phone. Her thighs trembled as she walked, and she knew it would be a while before her strength was back in full. If Rick turned up now, she would be at a significant disadvantage, even armed. He would be armed too.

Then she heard coughing behind her and turned to see Mrs. Benton sitting up slowly, pressing a hand to her head. "What's happening?" she asked in a shaking voice. Then she looked down at her torn clothes and the dried blood on her chest and screamed.

"Shh, it's okay, you're okay," Sadie said, going to the woman's side and kneeling down next to her. The sudden movement nearly made her throw up again. The old woman gazed up at her in shock.

"Sadie? What's going on? Where has the man gone? Did he do something to me?" Mrs. Benton was shaking all over and Sadie caught her hands, rubbing them as she felt how cold they were. The fire had gone out and with the door splintered open it was freezing inside the little cabin. Sadie took off her parka and draped it around Mrs. Benton's shoulders.

"Yes, he drugged you," Sadie told her bluntly and the woman gasped in horror. "A bear did that to you. I managed to shoot at it and scare it off before I passed out. That man—his name is Rick Bonsor—staged the recent bear attacks that have been happening around here. He's evil, and we need to get out of here before he comes back. That's what we're going to do. I just need you to sit here and get warm, okay?"

Mrs. Benton nodded mutely, looking terrified.

"Okay," Sadie said softly. "I'm going to call you an air ambulance, and then I'm going to call the sheriff. Then you can tell me how to get the fire going and we can get some heat in this place."

"What about the man coming back?" Mrs. Benton asked. She was still shaking. Sadie couldn't leave her on her own like this, and she was in no fit state to go prowling around in the dark. They were going to have to take their chances with Rick.

"I'll kill him," Sadie said in a voice devoid of emotion. Mrs. Benton looked at her and Sadie wondered if she had shocked the old woman.

"Good. You do that, dear," Mrs. Benton said.

Then they heard footsteps on the porch. Human ones.

Knowing that it could only be Rick, Sadie braced herself and trained her gun at the doorway. Her vision began to blur a little around the edges. *Not again, not now,* she prayed.

It was at that moment that Rick entered, and Sadie lost the element of surprise as his mouth dropped open and he took in the fact that the two women were alive and more or less unharmed.

"We meet again," Sadie quipped. She expected Rick to go for his gun, but instead he bolted back out of the cabin.

Coward, she thought contemptuously, running after him. Or at least, she tried her best to run on legs that didn't seem to want to obey her brain's commands. The aftereffects of the ketamine slowed her down and Rick was already in his Bronco as she stumbled down the cabin steps outside.

"Get the bastard!" Mrs. Benton screamed from inside the cabin and Sadie couldn't help but grin. Rick had started the engine of the Bronco and was about to pull away through the trees. Hoping the ketamine wouldn't affect her aim again, Sadie shot, allowing herself another smile, this one of triumph, as she blew out his front passenger tire.

The Bronco fishtailed, spinning out of control and crashing through the pine trees. Sadie raced after it. The truck slammed into a large pine and came to a standstill, and Sadie crouched, gun forward, waiting for Rick to come out. When there was no noise or movement, she started to move slowly toward the vehicle. With any luck the impact had knocked him out and she could take him down without a fight. She wasn't in any physical state for a full-on shootout now and she knew it.

Not that she wouldn't try. If ever there was a criminal she wanted to bring down with her bare hands, it was Rick Bonsor. The first man to pull the wool over her eyes the way he had.

She vowed that he would be the last.

Sadie was nearly at the Bronco when a gunshot sounded. She instinctively ducked before consciously registering the sound and felt a bullet go past her ear.

That was close. Clearly, Bonsor was both alive and lucid.

As another shot sounded, Sadie dived and threw herself under the Bronco, then waited. After a few moments, she heard the door open and saw Rick's feet step down. She shot him straight in the ankle and he fell to the ground, howling in pain. Seeing him bring his gun arm around she rolled out of the other side and jumped up, racing around the vehicle to see Rick staggering to his feet, holding on to the side of the Bronco.

Now, Sadie could see where they were properly. They were on the other side of the headwaters from where Carson's cabin stood. The pine trees came to an abrupt end just beyond them and the ground disappeared down a steep ravine. She remembered now playing here with Jessica, always being careful not to go too near the edge.

"Put your hands in the air," she ordered Bonsor. "And throw your weapon over the edge of the ravine."

Bonsor shook his head and laughed bitterly to himself, leaning against the Bronco with one hand, the other training his own gun on her. They were at a stalemate.

"I should have known not to underestimate you," he said. "What an elementary school mistake, not taking your gun. Do you know how much ketamine I gave you, Sadie? You should be out for the count."

"I'm tougher than I look, unfortunately for you. Now throw your weapon."

Rick met her eyes. He looked sad and also, she realized, admiring. "We could have been so good together," he mourned.

Sadie rolled her eyes. "Please," she said, her words dripping with sarcasm, "save me the romance. Drop your gun, Bonsor, or I'll shoot. You're in no position to argue."

Rick shook his head, and he lifted his chin defiantly. "No," he said stubbornly. "No, I won't come quietly so you can all paint me as the villain when you all are the villains. I was trying to protect the bears!" There was a note of hysteria in his voice. Sadie realized that he really did see himself as some kind of martyr. Sacrificing himself for the cause, just as he had sacrificed the poor mother bear and her cub.

"You're insane," she said flatly. Rick laughed, but it was a hollow sound, full of torment.

"Am I? Sadie, I think I'm the only sane one. I can't stand and watch this beautiful world of ours, and these beautiful creatures who have so much more right to it than we do, be destroyed by the follies of mankind anymore. One day, you will all understand that I was right, but by then it will be too late. I'm a man before my time."

"Do you actually believe your own bullshit?" Sadie asked him incredulously. Rick looked furious. "I mean, come on," she said, still keeping her gun trained on him and watching his own gun hand starting to shake. The blood from his wounded leg was staining the snow and she knew he must be in considerable pain. "Do you really think this is any kind of answer? There are plenty of conservation groups doing great things. You don't need to go around killing innocent people. What do you think you have achieved? Clarity will just build their resort elsewhere. You've done nothing but put yourself in prison for a very long time."

"I'm not going to prison," Rick insisted.

Then he shot at her.

With instincts honed by years of training and experience in the field, Sadie registered the movement of his finger on the trigger and threw herself behind the Bronco as yet another bullet went whistling past her ear, just a hair's breadth away.

She couldn't believe the bastard was still trying to shoot at her. She waited, then quickly leaned around the side of the Bronco and shot back, but Rick was trying to limp away, and her shot just missed him. He fired one back at her, but it went wide.

"Drop your weapon!" Sadie screamed. Rick tried to shoot her again, but unable to balance properly on just one functioning leg, he lurched sideways, tripped, and fell straight down the side of the ravine. She heard him howling in pain as he crashed against the rocks.

Sadie raced to the side and looked over. The drop was only a few feet here and shouldn't kill him. He lay by the banks of the river headwaters, on his back with his legs at a funny angle. Broken. There was no sign of his gun. He must have dropped it on his way down.

But that wasn't why he was staring at her in terror. Three large grizzlies were ambling toward him, sniffing the air as they scented his blood. Rick waved his hands at them, but it only antagonized the largest bear, who began to run toward him, roaring. Rick screamed.

"Help me, Sadie!" he begged. She should feel pity for him; no matter what he had done, being mauled by bears was a terrifying fate.

A fate he had happily left others to. Sadie felt no pity at all.

However, she was determined to operate on the right side of the law. As much as part of her wanted to leave Rick Bonsor to what seemed like a fitting end, she couldn't do it. That would make *her* the bad guy. Once a decision like that was made, she knew from bitter experience that there was no going back.

She fired off a few shots, randomly, and two of the bears scattered. The largest simply looked up and roared in her direction before sinking its teeth into Rick's shoulder. He screamed long and loud, the sound echoing around the ravine.

Sadie fired at the bear, hitting it in the haunch. It roared in pain before turning and running after its friends, leaving a trail of blood on the snow.

Sadie looked down at Rick, wondering if he would make it in the time that it would take her to go back to Mrs. Benton's cabin and call emergency services.

"Do you have a phone or radio?" she called down to him. Rick only groaned in response. He was losing a lot of blood.

"I do," came a familiar voice behind her. Sadie turned to see the sheriff.

"Cooper," she murmured. "Where the hell have you been? I could have used you a while ago."

"Looking for you, Price," the sheriff said, shaking his head at her in bemusement. "What the hell have you been getting up to now?"

They grinned at each other, before the sheriff pulled her into a long, tight hug.

CHAPTER TWENTY NINE

"Sadie!" Caz called through the apartment to where Sadie was sitting on the back porch, breathing in the crisp Alaska air. She was supposed to be finishing her paperwork on the bear case, but kept getting distracted by her thoughts.

"What is it?"

"Visitor for you...with the best hot chocolate in town," came a male voice behind her. Sadie smiled up at Sheriff Cooper as he sat down on the porch step next to her and handed her a steaming mug of hot cocoa from the bar's kitchen. Sadie sniffed at it dubiously. "There's no Irish Cream in this?" The cocoa Caz sold in the saloon was notorious for its potency.

"Maybe just a tiny bit." Cooper grinned. "You need it in this cold. Why are you sitting out here?"

"I think better in the cold," she said, waving her paperwork at him.

"You're a true Alaskan after all," he quipped, but Sadie didn't smile.

"Maybe," she acknowledged. She had only been back in the state a couple of months, but it was already starting to feel as though she had never been away. As though the last decade had just been an interlude in her life before she returned home.

"How is your father?" Cooper asked gently. "Any news?"

Sadie shook her head in frustration. "I was there this morning. He's been the same for days now. No change, just hanging in there on the edge of life. It's just like him, really." She tried to laugh, but the sound came out as more of a choke. Her father could stay in a coma for weeks, she realized, occupying the limbo between life and death. She was desperate for him to wake up in the hope that he would finish telling her what he knew about her sister's death, but there was another feeling too, one that took her by surprise.

She didn't want her father to die.

"If there's anything you need..." Cooper let his offer of help hang in the frozen air, looking uncomfortable. No doubt expecting Sadie to brush it off, she realized.

"Thanks, Cooper," she said instead, meeting his eyes. They stared at each other for a moment before the sheriff looked away with an embarrassed cough.

Something had shifted between them since Sadie's long night in Mrs. Benton's cabin, although she couldn't quite name what.

Or maybe she was just too scared to. Recent experiences hadn't exactly endeared her to the opposite sex.

"So," the sheriff went on in a more cheerful tone, trying to gloss over whatever had just passed between them, albeit for the briefest of moments, "when are you back at the Anchorage field office? Golightly will be thinking I've stolen his new agent."

"Monday," Sadie said with a sigh. It was Saturday.

"You don't sound happy about that," Cooper observed.

"It's what I came here to do," Sadie said lightly, not wanting to get into a conversation about why she was reluctant to leave the hinterlands and the station and get to her desk at the FBI office.

It occurred to her that she and the sheriff spent a lot of their time carefully avoiding things they didn't want to admit to each other.

"I can't keep running around out here with you hicks," she quipped. Cooper laughed in mock outrage.

"You're the one who grew up in these parts, Price. I'm a city boy. If there's a 'hick' around here, it ain't me."

They laughed together, the tension between them dissolving away. Sadie took a long swig of her cocoa and then coughed as her eyes watered. "You said a tiny bit of Irish Cream?"

Cooper shrugged. "Caz made them, not me."

"Well, that explains it." Sadie sipped gingerly at her drink.

"I was at the hospital myself this morning," Cooper told her. "Bonsor has given us a complete confession. He's in a pretty bad way; he'll be in there for a few weeks. Might have been kinder to just let the bears get him," he muttered darkly, in a way that suggested he wasn't thinking in terms of kindness at all.

"Has Garcia been released?" she asked. She wondered how both men felt, knowing the other was just down the hospital corridor a few rooms away. Cooper was using all of his state troopers on guard duty.

"Not yet. He'll post bail, but he will be ordered to stay well away from you. He doesn't deserve bail, attacking a federal agent. He'll get the book thrown at him for that."

"I doubt he will try to come anywhere near me again," Sadie said with a grin. "The worst injury I gave him was to his ego."

"Maybe he will think again before he tries to bully anyone else."

"I doubt that," Sadie murmured. Did bullies ever really change? Once again, she thought of her father, who had so terrified her as a kid, lying wasted and forgotten in a hospital bed.

"Bonsor got what he wanted anyway," Cooper went on. "Clarity Land Development won't be going ahead with the resort. And a lot of people have left the area. I'm sure you've seen it in the news. There is a group of eco-terrorists trying to claim Bonsor as some kind of martyr for the cause. Pushed to do awful things because of the crimes of the rest of us...you know the sort of thing."

Sadie shook her head. She was still stunned at the outcome of this case and at who—or rather what—Rick Bonsor had turned out to be. "I don't watch the news," she said. "But no, it doesn't surprise me. It's like how the worst serial killers always have fans—often female ones, too. People are attracted to the dark side, until they actually come face to face with it, that is."

She had to stop herself from visibly shuddering as she remembered the sensation of being physically helpless, waiting to be eaten. It would be a long time before she stopped reprimanding herself for missing Bonsor as a suspect.

Cooper seemed to read her thoughts. "Don't beat yourself up about Bonsor," he told her. "I didn't suspect him either. He was a lot cleverer than I would have given him credit for at first."

"Yeah, but at least you weren't considering actually dating him," Sadie muttered, feeling nauseous at the thought. She always thought of herself as naturally wary where men were concerned, too accustomed to seeing the absolute worst of what people were capable of to be able to really trust anyone or take them at face value, so her failure to recognize the darkness in Bonsor was still bothering her. But then, Rick was so convinced that he was the good guy that perhaps it had made it easier to miss. As Sadie had thought before, perhaps an idealist who was prepared to do anything for their ideals was even more dangerous than the most sadistic of criminals.

"Well, your taste in men is horrendous, Price, I'll give you that." Cooper's joke cut through her morbid thoughts, lightening her mood.

"It wouldn't be the first mistake I've made with the opposite sex," Sadie acknowledged, "but it might be the worst. Oh well, it was a good learning experience, I suppose. It's easy to think that as an expert, you're immune to being manipulated or taken in by a predator. But I guess the truth is that none of us are immune."

Cooper shrugged. "Well, I might not have suspected him as the killer," he said, "but I never liked him from the beginning. Right away I thought there was something slimy about the guy."

"Really?" Sadie teased, glad that they were back to being able to banter with each other. "Because I just thought that you were jealous," she laughed.

But her joke fell flat. Or perhaps it was too close to the truth to be comfortable. She watched the sheriff's face flame red even as his expression shut down and he looked away, staring over at the mountains in the distance.

"Cooper...you *were* jealous," she said, her words hanging between them in the crisp air. Cooper narrowed his eyes and refused to look at her. He seemed suddenly unable to speak and Sadie immediately wished she hadn't spoken. They were about to cross a line that had been unconsciously drawn between them, and she didn't know what the fallout would be from that.

Sadie was about to stand up and offer him a top-up of his cocoa, anything to change the sudden atmosphere between them so they could pretend that little exchange hadn't just happened, when Cooper coughed again and then looked at her intently, a serious expression on his face. There was something else too—almost a shyness.

Sadie knew what was coming and she felt her stomach twist in panic. All the reasons to cut the sheriff off before he could say something that couldn't be taken back, and would forever alter their professional relationship, raced through her mind.

Yet now it was she who seemed unable to speak.

"Sadie," Cooper said, using her first name for once, "I know this probably isn't the right time, but I was wondering if, maybe when all this has blown over, you would let me take you out for dinner?"

She stared at him. Taking in his clever hazel eyes, full lips, and rugged, tanned face. Wondering how she could ever have looked twice at Rick Bonsor when she had this man by her side every day.

Thinking of the best way to say no and let him down gently, because it couldn't happen. There were a hundred good and sensible reasons why she and the sheriff should never cross that line. She reminded herself of them regularly.

She had to say no, of course.

Yet she wanted to say yes.

Sadie was about to speak, not entirely sure herself what she was about to say, when her phone suddenly rang in her pocket, loud and shrill. She jumped, startled, and the moment was over.

Cooper stood up, knocking back his drink as Sadie answered her cell phone.

It was the hospital.

"Ms. Price?" It was the nurse who had been attending to her father, and now Sadie was holding her breath for a different reason.

"It's me. Is something wrong with my father?"

There was a pause and Sadie braced herself for the news that she was about to hear, knowing that this had been coming since the moment her father had gone into cardiac arrest. Knowing also that with him died her last chance of ever finding out what had happened to Jessica.

"Quite the opposite," the nurse said. "He's woken up. He's still incredibly weak and his vitals aren't great, so we can't be sure of anything yet, but is he awake and he's lucid. In fact, he's asking for you with some urgency."

Sadie let out a loud exhale, amazed to feel sudden, hot tears stinging her cheeks.

"I'll be right there," she said and ended the call. Cooper laid a hand on her shoulder.

"Price," he said softly. "Is your father…?"

"He's awake," she said. Her hands were trembling. "He's asking for me."

"Come on," the sheriff said, back to his usual practical self. "I'll take you. You look too shook up to drive."

For once, Sadie didn't refute an offer of help, but simply nodded and followed him around the building into the saloon parking lot.

Her father wanted to see her. That could only mean one thing, because knowing the old man as she did, she doubted that he had woken up with a burning desire to reconcile with his youngest daughter before he died.

He was going to finally tell her the truth about her sister.

CHAPTER THIRTY

Sadie rushed onto the wing with the sheriff close behind her. He had offered to wait in the snowcat for her, but she had realized that she wanted him there. Of course, she had made the excuse that if her father had anything to say about Jessica then the sheriff should be there to hear it too, as he had made the decision to investigate the cold case.

As she approached her father's room, she saw the doctor standing outside. Her father's door was closed and as the doctor saw her coming toward him his face fell slightly.

Sadie slowed down. Something was wrong.

"Ms. Price," the doctor said in a heavy voice. Sadie stood still so abruptly that Cooper nearly ran into the back of her.

"He's dead, isn't he?" she asked, her voice sounding flat and odd to her own ears, as though it belonged to somebody else. The blood rushed into her ears and when the doctor spoke again it sounded as though he was speaking underwater. Sadie put a hand on the wall to steady herself, aware that she was going into a type of shock.

"I'm so sorry," the doctor said with the genuine yet practiced sympathy of someone who had to do this very thing far too often. "He had come around but was still physically very weak. While you were en route, he had another massive cardiac arrest. We tried our best to resuscitate him, but I'm afraid it killed him instantly. We did try to call you again but were unable to pick up a signal."

Sadie nodded, feeling numb. She looked at the sheriff, who was gazing down at her with concern, and had no idea what to say.

She didn't know how she was supposed to feel, or react, to this.

Her father was dead. Her last surviving family member.

Not that he had been much in the way of family, but all of a sudden, it occurred to Sadie that she was alone in the world. They were all gone. Her father. Her mother.

Jessica.

She shook her head to try and relieve the ringing in her ears, trying to gather her thoughts, which were suddenly scattered and incoherent. A lifetime of memories assailed her. Her mother, sick and ill in this same hospital. Telling Jessica that she had to look after her little sister. Already knowing, even though her father had been nicer before her mother died, that he wouldn't be capable. She and Jessica, playing together in the cabin which had gradually become poorer and barer as their father's drinking progressed. Hiding under the bunk beds from his drunken rages, while Jessica pleaded with him to calm down. Jessica applying arnica to Sadie's bruises where her father had beaten her, again.

The morning that Jessica had disappeared. Her father, sinking into reclusiveness, drinking more and more. He never raised his hand to her again—Sadie was a teenager now and already capable of physically defending herself against him—but just ignored her instead. Apart from the times he expressed his disgust that she had been the one left alive. Not her mother or sister.

She had hated him. So why did she now feel so bereft?

Other, more complicated memories surfaced. The time when she had caught her father staring at her when she was around thirteen, an uncharacteristically soft look on his face. "You look so much like your mother," he had told her. Memories of being swung up on his shoulders when she was tiny, laughing gleefully down at her mother and Jessica.

The unmistakable pride in his voice last week when she had gone to his cabin, and he had asked her about breaking that guy's nose. The sudden relief in his face when he had finally agreed to tell her what he knew about Jessica's disappearance and subsequent death.

All gone.

Cooper was talking to the doctor. She blinked, dragging herself back into the present.

"He's still in there. You can have a few moments with him," the doctor was saying to her. "I believe the nurse wanted to speak to you too."

Sadie nodded again at him, watching as the doctor walked away, on to his next patient. She looked dumbly at Cooper, trying to process what she had just been told.

"The nurse wants to speak to you," Cooper repeated. "The waiting room is just over there. Or, if you wanted to see your father, he's still in his room."

Sadie nodded again. She seemed to be incapable of speech.

"I'll wait in the waiting room for you," Cooper told her.

"No!" Sadie blurted out. "Please," she whispered with an uncharacteristic vulnerability that seemed to move Cooper deeply, "will you come in with me?"

"Of course," the sheriff said without hesitation. He opened the door to her father's room for her and Sadie walked in, holding her breath.

Her father looked exactly the same as he had when she had visited that morning. Frail and ill, lying still in his bed, but there was nothing to signify that anything had changed, other than the fact that the tubes in his nose had been removed and the sound of the machines had stopped.

Sadie stood by his bedside as Cooper kept a respectful distance at the door. Her initial shock now dissipating, Sadie took a deep breath. She touched her father's forehead, feeing the cold chill of his skin. She wished that things could have been different, but they hadn't been. An eerie acceptance settled over her. He was gone, and it felt as though her hatred and anger had died with him.

In a strange kind of way, she was free.

But it was a bittersweet freedom. She could feel the weight of everything left unsaid and unresolved, but in a detached kind of way, recognizing that things were unlikely to have ever been resolved between her and her father. Perhaps this was the best ending between them that she could have hoped for. He too would have preferred this, rather than continuing to waste away from cancer.

There was just the matter of Jessica. The mystery of her sister's murder had lain on her shoulders for fifteen years, and until a few days ago her hopes of solving it had been renewed. She wasn't ready to let that go, even if she was ready to let the rest die with her father.

But what choice did she have? She sighed in frustration and looked up at Cooper. The compassion in his eyes nearly floored her and she realized something in that moment; the sheriff was her friend, and they really cared about each other. She couldn't afford to jeopardize that by letting anything romantic develop between them.

He meant too much to her.

Perhaps her father's timing hadn't been so bad after all, she thought wryly, thinking of how they had been interrupted on Caz's porch.

"Thanks for coming with me, Cooper."

"Of course," he said simply.

"I wonder what the nurse wanted."

Right on cue, there was a light knock on the door and the nurse entered.

"I'm so sorry," she said to Sadie. "It was so sudden."

"Thank you for all you did for him," Sadie said. "The doctor said you wanted to see me?"

"Yes," the nurse said briskly. "Your father left a note for you."

"A note?" Sadie took the folded piece of paper the woman was now holding out to her.

"Yes. When he came around, he was asking for you. Then he asked for a pen and paper and said to make sure you got this. It was almost as though he knew he was about to go. I do see that sometimes, you know. Almost as soon as he gave it to me, he went into cardiac arrest. I don't know how legible it will be though, I'm afraid. He was very weak, and his hands were shaking."

"Thank you," Sadie murmured, not moving. Taking her cue to leave, the nurse went out without another word, shutting the door behind her. Sadie looked again at the sheriff.

"Do you think…?"

"Open it," Cooper suggested. "Or if you want me to drive you home so you can be by yourself?"

Sadie shook her head. She looked at the paper in her hand as though it was a bomb about to go off. Could her father have written down whatever it was he had been about to tell her that morning in the cabin? After all this, did she finally have the missing key to her sister's death?

Or was it just a farewell note from a dying, repentant man? Afraid of having her hopes dashed once again, Sadie could barely dare to read it. She held the piece of paper out to Cooper.

"You do it," she said. The sheriff hesitated but then took it from her. As Sadie watched him, holding her breath, he unfolded it slowly and started to read. Then he frowned heavily.

"What is it?"

"It's not a note," he said slowly. "It's a map."

"A map? Let me see." Sadie held out her hand for the paper and Cooper passed it to her, standing beside her and looking at it with her from over her shoulder.

Sadie looked at the message from her father. As Cooper said, it was a map. Crudely drawn, but nevertheless an unmistakable rough map of part of the Anchorage hinterlands, with a few local landmarks for clarification.

And down in the right-hand corner was an unmistakable sign.

A large, dark X.

156

NOW AVAILABLE!

ONLY ONCE
(A Sadie Price FBI Suspense Thriller—Book 4)

When a body is found strung up on the crane of an offshore oil refinery on the Alaskan coast, FBI Special Agent is called in to investigate the suspected work of a serial killer. Against the stormy seas and brutal elements, she soon realizes there's more to this bleak landscape than meets the eye.

ONLY ONCE (A Sadie Price FBI Suspense Thriller) is book #4 in a chilling new series by mystery and thriller author Rylie Dark, which begins with ONLY MURDER (book #1).

Special Agent Sadie Price, a 29-year-old rising star in the FBI's BAU unit, stuns her colleagues by requesting reassignment to the FBI's remote Alaskan field office. Back in her home state, a place she vowed she would never return, Sadie, running from a secret in her recent past and back into her old one, finds herself facing her demons—including her sister's unsolved murder—while assigned to hunt down a new serial killer.

What seems like a straightforward case quickly embroils Sadie in an international territorial dispute, bringing in multiple agencies and countries and further complicating her investigation.

After a rabbit hole of dead ends, Sadie uses her brilliant mind to think of something no one else has—and another body—and a shocking twist—may just catch her off guard.

But in this stormy wilderness, in the thick of winter, does Sadie have any hope of finding him before it's too late?

An action-packed page-turner, the SADIE PRICE series is a riveting crime thriller, jammed with suspense, surprises and twists and turns that you won't see coming. It will have you fall in love with a brilliant and scarred new character, while challenging you, amidst a barren landscape, to solve an impenetrable crime.

Books 5 and 6—ONLY SPITE and ONLY MADNESS—are also available.

Rylie Dark

Debut author Rylie Dark is author of the SADIE PRICE FBI SUSPENSE THRILLER series, comprising six books (and counting); the MIA NORTH FBI SUSPENSE THRILLER series, comprising three books (and counting); and the CARLY SEE FBI SUSPENSE THRILLER, comprising three books (and counting).

An avid reader and lifelong fan of the mystery and thriller genres, Rylie loves to hear from you, so please feel free to visit www.ryliedark.com to learn more and stay in touch.

Made in United States
North Haven, CT
16 February 2022

16173114R00095